# QUITE POSSIBLY TRUE

# QUITE POSSIBLY TRUE

## A FREEMAN UNIVERSE STORY

### PATRICK O'SULLIVAN

dunkerron press

A Dunkerron Press™ Book.

# BOOKS IN THIS SERIES

# 1

---

Ciarán had known this day was coming. They had planned for it together, and spoken their parting words, some in the ship's mess, some in private, all well in advance, fearful that some last-minute emergency might rob them of the opportunity in the morning.

The night had passed peaceably and without event, and now there they were, all but the ship's captain, Agnes Swan, who had said her goodbyes brusquely during first-shift dinner the night before.

Swan remained at her post alone, having chased Maura and Ko Shan off the bridge with a fusillade of words. He'd heard the final salvos of the engagement from the corridor. The navigator and the sensors operator walked beside him toward the boat bay, hands stuffed in the pockets of their midnight-blue utilities, their steps quick and nearly silent.

The boat bay seemed unusually cold this morning. Ciarán doubted it was the temperature that had changed, but rather his thoughts. He stood at the back of their little going-away throng so as not to tower above the others and block their view, and so that he could have a quiet word with Engineer Hess.

They each stood as they'd entered, their backs to the boat bay blast doors, the League planetary-occupation shuttle crouching, blocky and businesslike, in the near field, a pair of second-epoch League shuttles lurking in the distance, tiny two-person machines, as ancient and strangely alien as the matte-black hull of the ship itself.

A pair of Freeman longboats rested near the boat-bay iris. *Quite Possibly Alien*'s own utility vessel lay dark and idle, all the last-minute activity centered around the surviving longboat from the captured pirate vessel, Truxton's *Golden Parachute*.

Mr. Gagenot also hung back because of his height. If Ciarán wished to compose a still image of *Quite Possibly Alien*'s remaining crew he couldn't have done a better job arranging them. He thought he might do just that, capture an image, later, once they were all returned to full health and reunited in Contract space. Even Wisp was behaving herself, sitting in front of the group as close to Mrs. Amati as he had ever witnessed. The big cat swished her tail once and yawned, fangs gleaming like diamond.

He had offered to send Wisp to Trinity space with the merchant captain, as a symbol of her authority, he'd told her, but in truth as a protector and ally. With Carlsbad out of action and Pilot Konstantine occupied with ship's duties, the merchant captain would be on her own once they moored at Trinity Station.

Wisp, however, did not like this idea and had refused to leave his side. Mrs. Amati, the merchant captain's usual companion on such missions, had volunteered to take Wisp's place. Aoife would have none of it, and in any case she'd no intention of separating the ship's cat from the ship, or taking the ship's weapons officer to a known and friendly port on a mere suspicion of danger. *Quite Possibly Alien* was heading into a war zone, and Mrs. Amati's place was with the vessel and crew.

A cloud of reaction mass enveloped the longboat as its thrusters ran through their full range of motion and Konstantine completed the last of the preflight tests. Pungent tendrils drifted their way and began to disperse as the longboat slowly lifted on repulsers alone. *Quite Possibly Alien's* boat-bay window opened like a vast eye and the longboat carrying Merchant Captain Aoife nic Cartaí powered free of the vessel's hull.

The merchant captain was bound for the captured vessel, Truxton's *Golden Parachute*, along with Pilot Helen Konstantine, in a rare good mood, and Cargo Master Carlsbad, in cryogenic suspension.

Also on board the longboat as cryogenically stored cargo was Ciarán's former Academy roommate Seamus mac Donnacha, until recently merchant apprentice aboard *Golden Parachute*, and until more recently still, host to a "terrifyingly malevolent mind parasite requiring immediate and forceful separation from his person."

Aoife nic Cartaí had instructed Ciarán to enter that precise phrase into the ship's log as a bloodless and incomplete description of a series of events that had left Carlsbad in need of emergency medical attention, Aoife in command of a captured pirate vessel, and Ciarán mac Diarmuid in charge of a sentient starship charitably described as mad, a crew most frequently described as pirates, and a thousand bloodthirsty Huangxu soldiers quite accurately described as cannibals.

All in all, exactly the sort of apprentice cruise he'd expected never.

Of course, as apprentice cruises his had turned out better than Seamus's. It was doubtful that Seamus would survive the superluminal transitions between Gallarus and Trinity space. The risk was worth it though. If Seamus remained here he would surely die, either of natural causes, or at the order of *Quite Possibly Alien's* ship's minder, a synthetic intelligence whose values weren't even vaguely human, but whose decision-making process was elegantly simple:

*Poke it.*

*Is it a threat to the League?*

*If so, kill it.*

*If uncertain, kill it.*

*Else, wait some unexplained amount of time and poke it again.*

It didn't help Ciarán sleep knowing that the ship's minder, laboring under outdated assumptions, had come within an instant of scouring all life from Freeman space, not as a final, desperate measure, but *purely as a precaution.*

Ciarán glanced at Engineer Hess. "Well?"

"You were right," Hess said. "I did find a problem. If I hadn't run a diagnostic the longboat's primary drive would have glitched. The repairs would have taken until tomorrow morning at the earliest."

And Merchant Captain Aoife nic Cartaí would have yet been aboard *Quite Possibly Alien* and thus still in command.

Ciarán didn't want the merchant captain anywhere near him tomorrow. He didn't want any of his comrades near him tomorrow either, but he'd thought it through, and getting Aoife off the ship and the crew's fate tied to his own was the best he could do. Tomorrow was noted in Ciarán's personal calendar as the Day of Remembrance, what some called the Day of Obligation, but which Ciarán thought of as the Death Day. It was the anniversary of his mother's death, and as she'd been born in the League, and old-fashioned in her ideas, and in her dying hours impossible to refuse, she'd roped Ciarán into honoring the ancient ritual with a promise. She had failed to mention that there were side effects to the ritual, effects that might appear coincidental to an objective observer, but which Ciarán knew were not.

He watched the boat bay wink shut, and in that moment Ciarán mac Diarmuid became merchant-in-charge aboard the vessel. Every life aboard *Quite Possibly Alien* became his to protect. They would remain his responsibility until Aoife nic Cartaí stepped aboard once again.

By Freeman contract and custom, the crew of a Freeman vessel were considered an extension of the merchant's person. Any offense against the ship or the crew was also an attack on the merchant. Perhaps that fact might buy his comrades some protection from the chaos tomorrow would bring. It wasn't much of a plan, but it was a plan he could execute.

"How'd you know to check the drive?" Hess said.

"The law of coincidences."

"That there are no coincidences?"

"That's just a saying. I'm talking about the iron law. You and I need to be on our toes tomorrow, and the rest of the crew as well. Spread the word, because tomorrow only comes once every few years."

CIARÁN ENTERED the merchant's day compartment, a small workplace jammed between the bridge proper and the communications cubby. The arrangement reminded him of the configuration of a typical Freeman merchant vessel, which is why he'd emptied out what had until recently been a storage closet and rechristened it the merchant's day compartment. He couldn't very well conduct ship's business from the merchant apprentice's berthing compartment, and he absolutely would not take up residence in the merchant captain's quarters, even though she had emptied the compartment of her possessions and ordered him to do so.

Move there he did, shortly before Aoife boarded the long-boat for Truxton's *Golden Parachute*. Once their farewells were said and the longboat had cleared the hull, he promptly executed his first order as merchant-in-charge, commanding the merchant apprentice to return his belongings to the merchant apprentice's berthing quarters.

He carried his bug-out kit to the merchant's day compartment. Wisp followed him in and padded around the compartment, and not finding a bunk, she glared at him accusingly before silently padding away.

He dropped his bug-out kit beside the worktable before closing the hatch. He took a seat and gazed at the deckhead. One of the ship's spidery luminaries had installed itself above the worktable. It could cast a pleasant, shadowless light if it wanted to. Or it could drop to the worktable and stab a spidery limb into his eye socket if it wanted to.

So far the overhead lamps hadn't turned mutinous. They had proven homicidal, however, while repelling boarders. He suspected the devices answered to the ship when providing illumination and to the ship's minder when providing perforation.

"Ship," he said.

"I am here," *Quite Possibly Alien* replied. The ship's voice seemed to come from everywhere and nowhere.

"Please ask Ship's Captain Agnes Swan to come to the merchant's day compartment."

"I have done so," the ship said.

Ciarán waited.

And waited.

He drummed his fingers on the worktable. "Ship."

"I am here."

"Please ask the ship's captain if she knows where the merchant's day compartment is."

"I have done so," the ship said.

"And?"

"And she bloody well does know."

"Her words, I take it."

"That is so."

"Sxipestro," he said.

"I am here." When the ship's minder spoke, it felt exactly as if it were speaking inside his head.

He didn't like that sensation. It felt like an invasion of privacy, so Ciarán made it a practice to always speak to the minder aloud, even though it had assured him there was no need.

"I'd like to talk to you about tomorrow and get your opinion on an object."

"Then do so."

"I will. But first I have a question regarding the function of this vessel."

"Go ahead."

"Can the ship monitor Agnes Swan's movements and disable any equipment she attempts to use?"

"It can't."

"Oh."

"But I can."

"I don't want to do anything that would endanger the ship or crew."

"You just want to irritate her."

"Until she comes here for a chat."

"Why not go to her?"

"Because if I'm merchant-in-charge then the crew needs to act like it."

"Including the ship's captain."

"Especially the ship's captain. If I'm going to get pushback I need to know it on day one."

"I would say you already know that."

"So would I. But I want it out in the open where I can deal with it."

"If I do this and she asks for an explanation?"

"You're aware that the merchant captain has been monitoring and censoring the crew's inbound communications."

"I am. I wasn't aware that you were."

"She mentioned it while on Gallarus, at the very last minute. Not what the messages were, specifically, but that they were the sort that might cause the crew to have second thoughts about the mission. That as merchant-in-charge it was up to me to decide whether to release them or not, and when."

"You think she was wrong to withhold the messages."

"I don't think that. I think it would be wrong for me to withhold them."

"Because you have different values."

"Not that I can tell."

"Do you not think the merchant captain had good reason to withhold the crew's messages?"

"At Ambidex? Maybe. But not now. There's too much at stake. No one is backing out no matter what is in those messages. Not after what we've been through. We're in this together all the way."

"And you believe the rest of the crew feels the same."

"I believe they will."

"And Ship's Captain Swan?"

"One of the messages was addressed to her. I'd rather not have this discussion with her in public."

"But you think that irritating her into meeting with you in private will set the appropriate tone."

Swan hated it when he cornered her in her cabin. They'd not got off to a good start, and despite occasional agreement, butted heads on nearly everything.

"I asked nicely first."

"I take it you've reviewed the messages."

"All of them but the one addressed to me. If it really is the sort of message that could make me abandon the mission I don't want to know about it on the first day of a new job."

"A job that might prove too much for you."

"A job that *is* too much for me if I have to do it alone. I need willing engagement and quality advice. When it comes to the crew there are only two people with the command experience I lack."

"Major Amati and Ship's Captain Swan."

"The merchant captain believed both of them might leave the ship at Ambidex if they viewed these messages."

"Then you should continue to withhold the messages."

"That would be easier. Where is Agnes now?"

"She is exiting her stateroom refresher."

"Then I guess it's safe to start messing with her."

"I have been 'messing with her' this entire time. Why else do you think she is exiting the refresher?"

"Ship," Ciarán said.

"I am here."

"Please inform the ship's captain I expect her to arrive clean and presentable, and that she should take whatever time she needs to see that it is so."

"She is on her way," *Quite Possibly Alien* said.

AGNES SWAN ENTERED the merchant's day compartment like a black cloud wrapped in Imperial red and gold. The leaping gold lions on her Huangxu skinsuit looked practically peaceful compared to the ship's captain herself. She folded her lanky frame into the chair across the worktable from him. Her jaw worked as she glared at him.

Ciarán stood, stepped out from behind the worktable, and brushed past her. He could have asked her to close the hatch but it would have come out of his lips as a command, and that wasn't the relationship he needed with the ship's captain.

Hatch closed, he returned to his seat. If anything she seemed to be getting more worked up by the minute.

He leaned forward and looked her in the eye. "Why weren't

you at the merchant captain's send-off?"

"Someone needed to keep watch."

"On a conventional vessel, that would be so. But there is the ship, and the ship's minder, and they're never more than a word away. Together they have been keeping watch over this vessel for more than two thousand years."

"While buried beneath a glacier. Perhaps if someone responsible had been in charge that interment might never have occurred."

"A fair point." He nodded and steepled his fingers, elbows on the worktable. "You were missed, that's all."

She stared at him, the muscles of her jaw continuing to flex.

He stood and walked to the hatch. "There's a message that should have been delivered to you at Ambidex and wasn't. I've forwarded it to your message queue."

She pivoted in her seat and glared up at him. "And you ordered me here to tell me this?"

"I didn't order you. I asked you. I wanted you to know you're a valued member of the crew and that I would hate to see you leave us."

"Are you threatening me?"

He was a large man, and in the best physical shape of his life. He could see how he might appear threatening. But physical threats didn't matter to people like Swan. She judged others by the same measures she judged herself. By their clarity of purpose and the depth of their resolve. And by their intellect, first and foremost. That he would never meet her standards was a given.

He looked her in the eye. "I'm not clever enough for that."

She stared back at him. "Show me this message."

He stepped away from the hatch and let out a long, slow breath. "I will."

And he did, the newly installed workstation waking at a touch.

She gazed at the workstation's display. There were three still frames, shot as if from cover, showing three Huangxu Eng and a Leagueman on the arcade of a station. The Leagueman and one of the Eng were handcuffed. Dried blood caked the side of the Huangxu Eng's face and neck. He was missing an ear. The two Eng escorting the prisoners were carrying bang sticks and looked to be prodding them along.

Ciarán waited for her to lean back in her seat. "Do you know where these images were taken?"

"Peaceful Dawn Platform."

"In Huangxu space."

"Yes," Agnes Swan said. "Original Hundred Planets."

"Do you know who the men are?"

"My brother, of course. In shackles. The others... No."

"Is this apparent situation... surprising to you?"

"My brother is ship's captain aboard the *Rose*, Thomas Truxton's personal vessel. I can think of no reason he would visit a played-out asteroid mining platform, and only one reason he would be bloodied on the ear and in shackles."

"He's taken the Oath."

"He must have done, to be mutilated in such a way."

"You don't seem surprised."

"We've argued over the wisdom of such an action. We have lived and worked in Freeman space for more than three decades, standard. The topic has of course come up."

"What would you like to do?"

"Go after him, of course. Rescue him."

"As a Truxton captain that responsibility is his employer's."

"Given our recent experiences? I will not rely on Truxton."

"What help do you need?"

"As a favor from you? Nothing."

"If you've lived in Freeman space for thirty years then you know we don't do favors. I may be a Freeman whelp but I'm also the merchant-in-charge of a superluminal vessel. Not to mention the contract employer of a second superluminal vessel and its battle-hardened crew."

"Huangxu crew. They dare not lift a finger against the Emperor."

"It might be a local misunderstanding."

"It might. What do you want in exchange for your help?"

"You won't like it."

"You want me to do your bidding without question. Else you want me to resign."

"I want you to do your job. To follow customary orders from the merchant-in-charge, and offer your best advice to the merchant-in-charge, and to argue with the merchant-in-charge when you believe he is in error. And I want you to do that whether you like or respect the merchant-in-charge or not.

"If you can't do that then I don't want you to resign. I demand it. And you can go after your brother. Alone.

"This vessel is going to Contract space. And this crew is going to live up to the merchant captain's word. When that is done the merchant captain may make the ship and crew's resources available to you. Until that moment I will help you if I can, and make resources available if I can, and work with you to develop a plan, and support you when you present that plan to the merchant captain. If you can find a merchant who can offer you a better deal I suggest you do so."

"You know I can't."

"Then draw up an agreement with these terms and we will both sign it. Until that time you are relieved of duty for however long you need in order to consider your options and discover what you can of your brother's present situation. Use whatever communications resources you need. We will break orbit the day after tomorrow. Depending upon the navigator's solution we may be in range of a superluminal node shortly thereafter. Compose what messages you think appropriate and they will be sent."

"Superluminal transceiver time is expensive."

"So is finding a new ship's captain."

She stared at him.

"We don't have to like each other to do business," he said.

"We don't," she said.

"We're done here," he said. "Unless you want to say something."

"The merchant captain would have offered me sympathy for my family's loss."

"What do you think I just did?"

"This isn't an act," she said. "You are actually angry with me."

"Furious. But your disrespectful behavior toward the merchant captain is only the proximate cause. I have a lot on my mind and you aren't making things any easier."

"Merchant Apprentice Ciarán mac Diarmuid would never speak to me in this manner."

"That's because he wasn't responsible for the lives and honor of the ship and crew. If I screw that up I'd rather it be for something I did than for something I didn't do. So I'm not just thinking that you were out of line today. I'm telling you.

"I have three brothers, and we were all raised by a pair of sticklers. There was never any question at home. If the stove was red hot whoever touched it was getting burned. No exceptions. No excuses. If you know a better way to keep a family aimed straight, then I hope you'll share it with me. But until you do I'm going with what I know."

She stared at him. Eventually she stood. "Your hands are shaking."

"I know it. Have you ever had to dress down someone more experienced than you?"

"Not yet." She paused with her hand on the hatch. "I'll have that contract to you in the morning."

"Not tomorrow. I'd like it today, or if not, the day after tomorrow."

CIARÁN SLUMPED into his chair and scrubbed his palm across his forehead. "One down. I don't think I can do that again today."

"Then speak with Major Amati tomorrow," the ship's minder said.

"Can't. Tomorrow is the sixth anniversary of my mother's death. It's a major event."

"A major event for you."

"For me and everyone aboard this vessel. It comes with a ritual obligation. One that has nasty side effects."

"Side effects for you."

"For everyone aboard this vessel."

"Then go to the planet and perform the ritual. Speak to Amati afterward."

"That wouldn't help."

"Describe these consequences."

"Unlikely events occur. My friends and acquaintances suffer. I don't."

"How many times have these unlikely consequences occurred?"

"Every time I've performed the ritual."

"How many times have you performed the ritual?"

"Twice."

"Twice doesn't establish a pattern."

"A line only needs two points."

"And humans see patterns where none exist."

"Not in this case. That Leagueman, in the images Swan just viewed? I've met him, the last time I performed the ritual. What are the odds of that? And the messages for Amati, and Hess, and Konstantine. They're related too. To that man. To me. To the ritual. I know it doesn't sound rational. But it's true."

"Unlikely."

"But not impossible."

"Describe these occurrences."

"I won't. It's against Freeman custom to discuss one's past with another person."

There was a long moment of silence.

"You think to flatter me. Who wouldn't want to be *another person*? We are not so different, you and I. Let us be *friends*."

"What? No. It's hard *not* to think of you as a person. And anyway, we don't need to be friends to work together. I was simply stating a fact while trying to establish resonance. It's a fundamental technique straight out of the *Manual of Trade*."

"I am not a 'person.' It would defeat my purpose if I were. And I am most certainly not a peddler's mark."

"Neither am I a peddler. And I wasn't trying to flatter you. I was trying to establish a connection with you. One that could serve us both well."

"Such a connection would not serve me. It would ruin me."

"Maybe." *Or it might just make you less likely to murder everyone in Freeman space by accident.*

That was Ciarán's hope, anyway, and the principle reason he'd summoned the ship's minder in the first place.

Which was actually not the right way to think about what he'd done.

He had alerted the minder to the fact that he was aware of its constant monitoring of him and everyone else on board, and that he wished to communicate. Summoning the minder made it sound like he was in command, and he most definitely wasn't. He couldn't order the minder to do anything. But he could reason with it and convince it to do as he asked. Or he could argue with it and possibly convince it to do, not as he *asked*, but as he *wanted*.

"Point taken. You are not another person. You're not even remotely human. So I wouldn't be breaking with custom by sharing my past with you. I trust you will keep our conversation private."

"If it suits my purpose to do so."

"That's the price of your help? My private business yours to sell or trade away?"

"Again, you confuse me with a human, and a peddler this time."

"It's important I convince you. Tomorrow is serious business. People could get hurt."

"Then convince me."

"If I have to, I will."

The minder said nothing.

"So be it." Ciarán had discovered recently that the minder didn't really care what he said. It only cared what he did. Saying that he would do something didn't register with it. If he told it he would do two contradictory things, one right after another, it would act as if it hadn't heard him. It concerned itself solely with actions and their consequences, intended or otherwise. He figured that this was an important part of its inherent monstrousness. Motives didn't matter to it. It didn't concern itself with intentions.

He didn't think it could read his thoughts. But even if it could, it seemed to treat whatever he thought as noise until the thought became a deed.

He readied himself. He wasn't a natural talker, but he'd grown up around talkers, and he'd studied the art of trade, which was at its heart far more about listening than talking. But what talking a merchant did wasn't just blather, but well thought out, and designed to both inform and persuade.

Ciarán closed his eyes and counted to ten before he spoke. "Shall I begin?"

"Begin."

# 2

---

"This is not a seanscéal, but a true account as witnessed by my own eyes. So say I, Ciarán mac Diarmuid of the Oileán Chléire, Trinity Surface, Freeman Federation. Here is how it happened."

"Stop," the ship's minder said. "Define this foreign term."

"Seanscéal? It means 'old story.' Like a parable, or a fable, but generally more long-winded. It's like... entertainment, but with a message. There's a standardized form, which they use in schools, and there's the informal version, which isn't really a seanscéal in the classical tradition, but a way of getting around the not-waking-the-dead custom. I tell you a story, it's about people we both know, we can both recognize them from the story, but I don't use their names, but pseudonyms, or just 'yer man' or 'yer wan' for the characters in the story.

"Even if the people in the story hear it, or hear about it being told, they can't file intent, since it's just a story, and their names are not in it. It could be I'm telling an entirely different story about the same set of circumstances, where yer man stole a cow and yer wan went to war over it, for instance. And if you think the story is about you? Well, that's just your guilty conscience talking, isn't it?"

"Noted."

"Are you going to continue to interrupt and ask questions? I don't mind if you do, but I'd like to know up front. It matters to the telling."

"Is it a long story?"

"Short."

"Continue without interruption."

"I will." Ciarán wished the ship's minder had a face, or even a body to look at. He couldn't judge how it reacted to the story so he could adapt it as he went along. He supposed if the ship's minder didn't like the story the luminaire overhead could drop down onto the workstation and show its displeasure. But this wasn't a seanscéal related to the ship, so he didn't think it would do that.

"Here we go." He repeated the preamble because it would feel strange to just launch into the story without it.

# 3

---

This is not a seanscéal, but a true account as witnessed by my own eyes. So say I, Ciarán mac Diarmuid of the Oileán Chléire, Trinity Surface, Freeman Federation. Here is how it happened.

On the first anniversary of my mother's death there was a big do at our farm. Neighbors from all over the island came. It got a little wild, and Macer, that's my best mate, and his dad got into an argument, with Macer wanting to leave, and his dad wanting to stay, and the bad feelings between them boiled over on the dock where their boat was tied up.

Macer's dad took a swing at him and missed, and tripped on the new cleat my brother Tadhg had installed the day before, and plummeted off the dock, and hit his head on a stone that hadn't been there in the morning, I'd swear.

The water wasn't deep but he was floating face down and not moving. The water was a ways down from the dock but there was a ladder we used for swimming nearby. When my brother Mícheál tried to use the ladder, it finally finished its rusting through and parted beneath his feet. Mícheál clung on, and hoisted himself up, and both he and Tadhg went to fetch our skiff, as its gunnels were low to the water and it was easy to maneuver amongst all the tied-up boats and pilings. Someone had moved the little boat though, so it took them quite some time to find it.

They were gone for so long searching that the county coroner, who was also at the party, had some lads use a looped line and the hook of a gaff to fish yer man out, and lay him out on the dock, and soon pronounced him dead. He wrote out the death certificate on the spot, and handed it to my dad, who witnessed it, and then he handed it to the county clerk, who also witnessed it, and entered it into the county record via a handheld device.

I remember this part clearly because I'd never seen a handheld device that worked on the island. Later I learned that they'd spun up a new satellite array that very day, and that database entry was likely the first of its kind.

The Ellis, another of our neighbors, and a rival to Macer's dad in county politics, congratulated Macer, and all the men started calling Macer "the Gant," which was his family name, the title signifying he was senior of the family now that his dad was dead, and heir to the family estate, which wasn't a two-pig affair like our own farm, but the second biggest and wealthiest property on the island.

Macer was gutted at the death of his father, and though a strong man, he was on the verge of breaking into tears when he heard a sound he recognized.

His dead father had started snoring.

Some of the men poured whiskey down the dead man's throat and that roused him up lively, but it didn't stop the Ellis from calling Macer "the Gant" or the other men from asking Macer's dad what heaven was like, and were there other gombeen men there, or he the first.

I thought that was pretty funny, a gombeen man in heaven, but later I learned that the men had just said that because if they'd asked him what hell was like and he'd said, "It looks just like the mac Diarmuid place," my old da would have murdered him, dead or not.

Macer's dead father didn't think any of this was funny at all, and he thought it even less a laugh when the Ellis started talking about Macer marrying his daughter, now that Macer was a propertied man. The daughter was considered fair to middling in appearance but very fierce and clever like her father, and knowing Macer, if they'd married she'd be running the show, and the dead man knew that. There was an arrangement between the Ellis and Gant women years back, an agreement the two children would marry, and Macer's dad was widely known to oppose the idea, not on principal, as he claimed, but as a matter of pride.

It wasn't that Macer was weak minded, or weak willed, but Laura Ellis was exceptionally bright, and exceptionally fearless, and exceptionally organized like her old da, and I've heard from my brother Niall that she blossomed a year or two later, and now there isn't a lad on the island that courts a girl who doesn't compare her to the Ellis Og, and finds every other girl lacking in some dimension. The Ellis Og is what they call her now, but back then they just called her Laura, and it was Laura and Macer this, and Laura and Macer that, until Macer's poor old dead da rose up on his hind legs and shouted.

"You are all fools! The boy will not see a pingin from me, and not a hectare, but for that boggy strip his mother brought in dowry! So take your Laura and throw her away, for all I care. There'll be a fine young wife and a brace of bright-headed boys sleeping beneath that roof before I'm in the ground a week."

Macer stood there like he'd been struck by a meteor.

The Ellis laughed. "Would that be Macer's fine young wife and boys?"

"He hasn't the gumption. It would be my own, shipped over from the mainland," the dead man said.

Macer stared at the dead man.

The dead man stared at Macer.

And then the fight broke out.

That's all I have to say about the first time.

Except that it took Macer's dad nearly a year to get declared undead again, and in the meantime Macer had sold that boggy strip he'd inherited and the buyer had leased it to the Ellis for ninety-nine years, standard, and the last I'd heard Macer's dad was still trying to untie that knot.

And even though he was officially dead, Macer's dad hung about the place like a ghost, and made Macer's life miserable, also like a ghost, so much so that Macer got the bright idea to leave home for the Freeman Merchant Academy. He bought the study materials with the money from that land sale, and I helped him study, and I helped him send his application in, and I put my own application in as the postage was the same with or without, and the rest, as they say, is history.

All those coincidences, all on the same day, and all those people hurt.

And what do I get out of it?

Propelled into space, where I'd wanted to be all along.

And it happened again, the next time I performed the ritual.

Me, getting what I wanted and other people paying.

It's a bad day, the Death Day.

And that day is tomorrow.

# 4

Ciarán sat and waited. He'd made up that story last night out of true facts, just condensed and arranged in the way that the coincidences were nested three deep. It was the sort of story his dad and his cronies liked to tell, part conspiracy theory, part sting, part vigilante justice. He'd heard such seanscéalta thousands of times as a child and back then he'd found them impossible to follow.

When he'd watched the events of that evening play out, he realized that the men couldn't have hatched such a devious plan without a lifetime supply of such stories rattling around in their heads.

Macer's dad was a smart and powerful man. A successful man that had built a fortune with one calculated risk after another. And he'd been utterly played. It wasn't the drink alone that clouded his thinking, but his regard for his neighbors. He didn't know them at all, so high was his nose above them. But they knew him, having studied him from every angle.

That mistake had cost him a son, and a large part of his reputation.

Such a mistake by the ship's minder might cost Ciarán's

friends and family their lives. Everything Ciarán had told the minder about his mother's Death Day was a fact. It was a dangerous day for the ship and crew, and they needed to be forewarned. *And* everything he'd put into the seanscéal was there for a second reason. That was the beauty of the seanscéal. It could speak with two voices at once.

"Well?" Ciarán said.

"Well what?"

"What do you think?"

"Tell me about the second time."

"I'd rather not. People died and I don't like recalling it."

"They died because of this ritual you performed."

"I'm not claiming the ritual causes these coincidences. But I am certain that they occur around the time I perform the ritual. There could be another mechanism at work, and the two happen to be synchronized. It feels like the ritual is the trigger, though."

"Describe the ritual."

"I will if I have to, in the telling of the story. But I shouldn't have to. Can't you just believe me?"

The ship's minder said nothing.

"Fine, have it your way. I'll begin, just as soon as you tell me you're ready."

"I am ready."

Ciarán took a deep breath and let it out slowly.

Now he was ready too. He didn't want to tell this story. He'd thought about it for years and he still hadn't found a way to turn it into a seanscéal. If there was something to be learned from it he couldn't yet see it.

Someone tapped on the compartment hatch.

"Hold that thought." Ciarán stood and opened the hatch.

"You asked to see me," Mrs. Amati said.

"Will you come in and close the hatch?"

Mrs. Amati stood at attention, not strictly in a military

manner, but in the manner of someone who expects an assailant to leap out of the shadows at any minute. Ciarán hadn't noticed this aspect of Mrs. Amati's routine behavior before she'd begun leaping out of the shadows and assailing him as part of his self-defense training. She explained the technique to him, and even demonstrated it, repeatedly, but he still found it unnatural, and he imagined it looked unnatural when he did it. On Mrs. Amati it looked normal, though how much of that was down to the fact that she appeared composed as much from cybernetic augmentation as human flesh he couldn't say. She appeared ready and dangerous at all times. *Locked and loaded*, as she would say.

"Will you have a seat," Ciarán said. "There's something I need to ask you and something I need to show you on the workstation display."

She sat. "In that order?"

"In that order. There were a number of messages delivered to the vessel in Ambidex space that weren't forwarded on to the crew. One message was addressed to you. I'm going to ask you a question, and then I'm going to show you another message directed to the ship's general address, and then it'll be up to you to decide what to do with your own message."

"You're preparing me for bad news."

"I suppose I am."

"Then just rip the bandage off and let's move on."

"Are you still in the League military, either active duty or reserve?"

She stared at him. After a while she spoke. "I don't see how that is any of your business."

"It wouldn't normally be. And you've just answered my question. I imagine if I asked Hess or Konstantine I'd get the same non-answer answer."

"You'd have to ask them."

"I intend to."

She glanced at the deckhead. Noticed the luminaire. He could see the idea forming inside her mind and working its way to her face. *We're on the same team.*

She glanced at him and their gazes met. "There's a trap for people like me."

She shoved her mechanized arm into the light. "Military cybernetics are far superior to anything available on the commercial market. It's a thorny subject, and one I prefer to ignore rather than to dwell upon. But yes, I am still associated with the League. So long as I remain a reserve officer I get to keep the government-issued parts of me. The moment I resign my commission I'm less than half of what I am today."

"That doesn't seem right. Or just."

"Like I said, I prefer not to dwell on it."

"But the League might recall you to active duty should they wish to."

"I can't imagine they would want to. But it's theoretically possible."

"And if they did?"

"They'd contact me and tell me where to report."

"And would you? Report?"

"It won't happen."

"That's a yes. And not just because you're worried about what hardware you'd lose if you didn't."

Amati stared at him with both eyes, one human, one cybernetic. "I don't expect you to understand."

"You made a promise. And if you don't keep your word, who will?"

"Like I said, it won't happen."

"The ship is in receipt of three messages to three addressees, all three from the same originating address, all of identical length, all with identical metadata, all marked urgent."

"Hess, and Konstantine, and me. From Fleet Command on Brasil Station."

"From the War Department Office of Personnel on Columbia Station."

"Blast it."

"Now," Ciarán said. "What I have to show you. The message received on the ship's general channel."

"Has Aoife nic Cartaí seen this message?"

"She has."

"And that's why I'm only now getting my mail. Because she left the decision to tell me up to you. And you're telling me."

"Telling you. And Hess. And Konstantine, if she were here."

"Even though the merchant captain thought it better not to."

"She's more experienced than I am. More cosmopolitan. Born into a spacefaring family, with connections and a reputation to fall back on. She doesn't just see the world differently than I do. She lives in a different world. One where she has a choice of options and the brains and talent to choose between them."

"And you're going against all of that."

"I'm not. That would be stupid. But what I need and what she needs are different. And what I can afford to pay is different too. Maybe it's more, maybe it's less, depending on what you're looking for."

"I see."

"I'm not sure you do," Ciarán said. "Not if you think that more than half of your value to this vessel and crew has a serial number stamped on it."

Amati stared at him. "You've changed."

"You told me to rip the bandage off," Ciarán said. "I'm just following orders."

"Is that what Freeman merchants do nowadays? What they're told?"

"I wouldn't know, being but an apprentice."

Amati snorted.

"Well if I'm not a model merchant, it's down to the merchant captain. And it's down to you. Not your mechanical right arm, but your heart, and your mind. I figure anyone could teach me how to aim a weapon, and I'd listen. But where to aim it, and when? And when not? I rather feel that's a job for someone I can trust with my own life, and my own honor. You once told me that when in death ground—"

"You fight."

"Right. So that's what I'm doing. Except I'm not fighting an enemy I want to beat. I'm fighting a young woman who made a promise and kept it. Even if no one else around her did."

"And you want her to break that promise."

"I want her to stand up and declare her obligation met. And then I want her to make a new promise."

"To you."

"To herself." Ciarán watched her eyes. "There are two sides to every contract. Obligation flows both ways."

"Is that what you're offering? Obligation?"

"It's all I have."

He watched her flex the augmented fingers of her military-issue hand. A hand she would lose if she were forced to resign her commission to remain with the crew. He hoped there was another way, but he wasn't counting on it.

After a while she stood. "I'll talk to Hess. There's no need for you to deal further with this."

"Thank you."

"I'll let you know my decision tomorrow."

"Don't," Ciarán said. "The next day. Or not at all. All I need to know—"

"You'll know by watching me."

"That's the Freeman way," Ciarán said.

When Amati exited the compartment she closed the hatch behind her.

"You wanted her to view the message from the ship's general-address queue," the ship's minder said.

"I did, but it wasn't worth it to push. Now I'll have to find some other way to get her to view it."

"To what end?"

"I think she's telling the truth. But I'm not sure she's telling the whole truth."

"Based upon?"

"My self-defense training. Mrs. Amati knows a lot of unconventional techniques in stealth, and concealment, and in found-weapon fighting that don't seem very regular military. You've watched us. What do you think?"

"I have no opinion on the matter. Though I fail to see what this has to do with the message in question."

"I want to know if she recognizes anyone in the attached drone recordings."

"Because?"

"Because I need to know. It feels like I'm always in the dark, and there's something going on that others are keeping from me. And I'm tired of it. I can't make full decisions with half facts."

"And this *feeling* is based upon?"

"On experience." Ciarán leaned back in his seat and gazed at the deckhead. "We were going to talk about the second time I performed the ritual."

"You were going to talk."

"Do I have to do all the work?"

The ship's minder said nothing.

"So be it."

# 5

---

This happened on the third anniversary of my mother's death. By this time I'd been accepted to the Merchant Academy. As a first-term student I was told to arrive for orientation two weeks before the term began. What I wasn't told is that student housing isn't available until the term starts. I'd scraped together enough to pay for a ticket on the shuttle, tuition, room and board, and study materials, but that was all. Macer had blown off orientation, but I'm a rule follower, so I was up there, on the station, alone, and very nearly a pauper.

I was assigned a student advisor, and met with her in her office, a very comfortable setup designed to put new students at ease. She didn't have a desk she issued decrees from behind, but rather a U-shaped arrangement of two chairs and a sofa, all surrounding a low table that we hunched over casually, and chatted as equals, and it was from the sofa that she passed judgment. She told me, no, don't sit on the plush sofa next to her, but in a hard chair, across from her, with the table between us like a desk that hadn't grown up.

She said it wasn't uncommon for this temporary yet entirely predictable insufficiency of funds to plague the dumb kids from the bad homes, only she said it nicer. She explained that the Academy had found a way for such short-sighted unfortunates to cover their costs to the Academy before inevitably flunking out and plunging back down the gravity well like the rubbish they were. Again, said nicer, but said clearly.

She quizzed me about my life experiences and skills, and she did it in such a way that it didn't seem like she was delving, largely because she wouldn't have cared if I had burst into flame, so long as I did it after I'd vacated her office.

She didn't seem very pleased with my answers. I quickly realized it was because she was at least partly right. I didn't have any skills that were useful on a space station, not any that couldn't be done cheaper and faster by a machine or by a "real" Freeman, which meant anyone that had lived on Trinity Station since birth, like her.

While I didn't have any skills, what I did have was size, and reach, and persistence. It finally dawned on her that I was camping out in her office, and since I was a planetary hick destined for flameout there was nothing restraining me from reaching across her undesk, grasping her by her fashionable station-length hair, and flinging her into the corridor so I could stretch out on the nice couch she'd told me not to sit on. I didn't need to say a word. I could watch the narrative she'd invented about me play out behind her eyes.

Eventually she found a spot for me. There was a last-minute opening with a new firm called "Academy Muscle," which specialized in lifting and toting, the sort of cleanup and junk-removal work that wasn't worth automating. She didn't have any experience with them, the Merchant Academy hadn't used them before, but it was either them, or nothing.

I met with the owner, and it went okay, and he paid me a day's work in advance. I'd stored my duffel in a shuttle-terminal locker, but I still lugged my bug-out bag everywhere, so I had all I needed to sleep rough. He gave me a couple of shirts, signal-green ones that had the company name on them in erlspout and told me to meet up with the rest of the crew at the League-sector transit gateway in the morning. When I did we breezed through security: the owner, two young women, another man, and I.

I tried to make small talk but I wasn't very good at it back then, and they pretended not to understand me. They were all smaller than me but wiry and in great shape. They wore loose clothing, and even the blazing green shirts were loose on them, and while the shirts the owner gave me were the biggest he had, when I put one on it clung to me like a second skin. The sleeves didn't even come halfway to my elbow. There wasn't enough tail to tuck into my trousers. It felt like people were staring at me because people *were* staring at me. Imagine a gorilla and four weasels on the Trinity Station League Sector Arcade. Who is going to be looking at the weasels, even if they're wearing signal-green shirts?

The boss led us to the docking ring, but a very old part of the ring, one that didn't have mooring berths but had been converted into lockup storage by welding Freeman Freight Expeditor containers perpendicular to the ring. The FFEs stuck out like fingers from a palm but other than being welded in place and having their drive systems removed, they were just like every other FFE I've ever seen, capable of opening at each end and with active environmental systems, so you could store anything you wanted in them from ice cream to lava.

The boss said that the ring was being converted into standard mooring berths and all the stuff in these old lockups had to go. Some of them hadn't been opened in years and some of them were still used daily, just not by the leaseholder, which was him. If I saw anyone messing around with the FFEs I should run them off. They were squatters, and when he'd purchased the leases on the containers he'd bought the contents as well, and don't let anybody tell me different. If I needed to get rough to stop the stealing he was fine with that.

I asked him if he wanted to amend my contract to cover these expanded duties. He stared at me for a while before he told me to shut up and just do what he said.

The procedure was that he would enter the access codes and step back so we could do the rest. It wasn't very hard work and it was interesting. There was everything in those containers. There were musty mattresses, and wine that had gone bad years ago, and ten buckets full of sandy loam, which we had to dump out and paw through, and one of those wire puzzles that looked like any child could undo it, but when you tried you couldn't, only this one wasn't sized for hands playing, but meant to hang on a wall, or be worked by giants. Most of what was there was rubbish but not all of it. You'd think on a space station there'd be a premium for storage, and there was, but this was like Trinity Station's junk drawer, and even the humblest of homes had room for one of those.

It didn't matter what it was, we hauled it out and dumped it into one big pile. The boss toed through the stuff we piled up, and he moved some of the small stuff to other, smaller piles. If it was heavy or hard to grip and he wanted it moved, he told us where to pile it. The first big pile was for general disposal, and the smaller piles were for specialty recycling, and resale, and some of the stuff didn't go into the piles, but ended up stuffed in his pockets, or into a cargo bag he kept with him at all times.

There weren't a lot of people on this segment of the ring because it wasn't very convenient to get to, and it was, to put it kindly, shabby. I suspected the boss and his regular crew had invested a bit of Academy Muscle in driving the squatters away before the heavy work had begun. Every now and then someone would wander in but it wasn't more than a once-a-day interruption. I didn't like what I saw whenever that happened, but I needed the work and I had no reason to doubt the boss's claims of ownership.

We started at the spinward blast doors and worked container by container anti-spinward, except we skipped one FFE on the third day. The boss said because the access codes weren't working. He also said that all the FFEs were inactive leases, except later that afternoon I was pretty sure I heard cargo being loaded into the FFE we had skipped. Someone was using the outboard access hatch, had to be.

Squatters on the ring I could understand. But squatters with orbital cargo-handling equipment? That seemed unlikely. Either way, I was there for a paycheck. Mentioning something that might shut down the job didn't make a lot of sense. I did make sure to stand pretty far back when the boss was entering the access codes from then on, and to never open the containers myself, but to hang on to something and brace myself, just in case someone had left the outboard access hatch open by accident, or, now that I knew my coworkers better, had left it open on purpose.

I think if I'd been station-born I would have known that FFEs have safety interlocks to prevent just such occurrences. But then again, back home the Gant's brush-hogging bot had safety interlocks. That hadn't stopped their "factory-trained technician" from losing three fingers from her right hand.

Nothing bad had happened yet. The third anniversary of my mother's death was fast approaching and the worst stuff happened on the Death Day itself. Whatever we were really doing emptying those FFEs felt marginal at best, not because I knew of some custom or law we were breaking, but because the boss and the rest of the crew were acting like they knew.

Early the next day we skipped another FFE, and the next day we skipped another. Both times I heard loading or unloading activity coming from the containers, and the only way that could happen was if someone was working the container from the other end, in vacuum.

When I showed up for work the next morning, the transit gate between the Freeman and League Sectors was backed up halfway to the Guild Hall. The previously self-serve security gates were now manned by black-uniformed guards and they were asking for documentation.

I could see the boss and my coworkers on the League side of the checkpoint, and I shouted for them, partly to get them to wait, but mostly to let the boss know that I was at the meet-up point on time, because that meant he owed me a day's wages whether I worked or not. I was there, and ready to work, and that was the deal we'd made. I had it in writing on a data crystal in my pocket.

I shouted louder but they pretended not to hear. So I shouted louder still, and waved my arms. They could have heard me on Midpoint Platform I was shouting so loud, because I needed that job, and if I lost it I wouldn't find another. I didn't know anything, I didn't have any connections, and there wasn't a single task on Trinity Station that I could do as well as the most backward stationer's child.

Even the weasel clan was better at picking stuff up and putting it in piles than I was. It was like they were all possessed with the burning need to search between the cushions of every sofa and all I wanted was for them to get out of the way so I could pick it up and put it on the big pile before I cooled down and my triceps started to cramp.

It took forever to get to the front of the checkpoint line. I was in a hurry because even though I'd met the terms of the contract it would be a devil to prove it, and use up time and money I didn't have. I need to be working, not arguing, and the sooner I got to the job site the harder it would be to dock me for being late. I could afford to lose an hour. I couldn't afford to lose a day, or worse, lose the whole job as a no-show. I wasn't panicking yet but I was concerned.

I didn't have any government identification, as we didn't use it on the planet, and the only things close I did have were the contracts with the Merchant Academy and with Academy Muscle, and neither had my picture on it. So they pulled me out of line and sent me to another line, where they took my picture, and printed out a card, like a merchant license only red, which they said indicated I was entitled to work but not to live in the League Sector. I was in a hurry, so I just stuffed the card into my pocket and got back at the end of the long line, which was even longer now, and when I got to the front they scanned my card and let me through. I was seriously late by now, so I shifted my bug-out kit's straps higher onto my shoulders and got ready to run.

"You there," someone said. "In the green shirt."

He was another guy in uniform, except his uniform wasn't black, but gray.

I couldn't afford to be later still, so my need to earn and my natural tendency to follow the rules went to war, and when my stomach growled I knew who'd won. I had to get to work.

"You can't turn and look at me and then pretend you didn't hear me," the man said. "It's disrespectful."

"I'm in a hurry," I said.

"I can see that. I can also see that you're carrying a large pack, and look rather anxious and unkempt, and are a foreigner without proper identification, and the sort of person to contemplate ignoring a direct order by a duly appointed representative of the Crown. Given all these facts I am delighted to inform you that you've been selected for secondary screening."

The man waved to the black-uniformed guards manning the checkpoint. One simply stared at him. The second directed a rude hand gesture at him. At least it looked like a rude hand gesture to me, because it would have been on the Freeman side of the checkpoint.

Maybe the one-fingered salute meant something different in the League Sector. I thought about trying it out on him and going on my way, but it was like he was a mind reader.

"Running would be a mistake." His face had gone all still and his eyes all hard, and when my gaze met his it was like the time I'd surprised a wolf right after he'd buried his muzzle in a fresh kill.

"Good boy," he said. "Now hop to and give me your identification card."

I followed him to a table, and he stood on one side of the table and I stood on the other, and I handed him the card. He looked at it, and then he stuck it in his pocket and told me to dump the contents of my bug-out kit onto the table.

"I don't have time for this," I said.

"The longer we argue the longer it will take. Now please do as I ask."

I could tell from the cadence of his words that "please" wasn't something he said often. His uniform was nicer than the black uniforms of the checkpoint guards, and it had more badges and braid. I figured that meant he was more important.

The guards had weapons, though, and he didn't. But then, he was on the safe side of the checkpoint, and maybe he didn't need a weapon. Maybe he used people with weapons like people with weapons used weapons. By pointing and twitching his finger.

So I did as he asked, because I figured there was an upper limit to how long that would take, and I couldn't even guess how long it would take if I defied him.

There was a fair amount of stuff in my bug-out kit, and it mostly covered the table. He started pawing through it, separating it into piles, just like the boss had been doing with the stuff in the containers, but on a much smaller scale.

The first pile he made contained the most basic stuff in the kit: emergency rations, water, water maker, sleeping bag. To that he added the rest of my camping gear, including the half tent, which wasn't all that useful on a space station, but then that wasn't the purpose of a bug-out kit. It wasn't designed to keep you alive where you planned to go, but wherever you ended up.

He stared at the pile and muttered to himself. I could have wandered off just then and he wouldn't have missed my going. Except he had my personal stuff and I wasn't leaving without it, even if that meant I lost my job, or even if it meant I had to take the shuttle home, tail between my legs.

He picked up my field-reinforced gloves. "Mark One survival gauntlets, a mismatched pair. Very old. Very used. Very recently serviced."

He glanced at me and I shrugged. On the farm you either learned to fix it yourself or you did without.

He slid a glove on. Then he squeezed his other hand into the same glove and somehow managed to power it up. I didn't think that was possible, because you had to make a tight fist to work the power-up sequence. He then ran the gloves through a series of field extensions so fast I found it hard to follow. Most of the configurations were known to me but there were some I'd never seen before, and some that were entirely impossible with a single hand.

"The power of ten men," he muttered. "The power of ten squared, no prison can hold him. Charger sold separately."

He powered the glove down and withdrew one hand, then the other. He tossed the glove onto the pile.

He repeated the procedure with the second glove, only without the parody of that old hardhands advertisement. It, too, ended up on the pile.

He picked up my portable shovel. He racked the shaft to full extension and triggered it alive. The blade field glowed a flickering blue. A hiss just short of a roar spewed forth from the power supply. The blade was adjustable in shape from a trencher to a sharpshooter to a digging shovel and more. It kept its last-used form when powered on, and it sprang to life as a mucking scoop.

"Not very stealthy." He powered it off and ejected the power supply. He turned the power supply over and worked on the tiny control panel for a few seconds. He popped the power supply in and powered up the shovel and it was dead silent. The force blade glowed a steady blue. "Fixed if for you."

I had liked it the way it was. We used regular shovels on the farm, which weren't any louder than the heavy breathing of the operator. Up on the mountain I preferred a loud shovel, one that shouted here's a man with a sharp blade on the end of a long stick. Surprise rarely worked in your favor when everything you might meet was bigger, and meaner, and hungrier than you. The best way to deal with predators was to make it easy for them to steer clear. He hadn't fixed my shovel. He'd broken it.

He stared at the pile and rubbed his chin. "Infantry kit. Half of what you need to survive. Requires a partner." He glanced at me suddenly, and our gazes met and held for a disturbingly long time.

He tore his gaze away and returned his attention to the pile. "Working alone, then." He continued to paw through my belongings, and mutter, and add to the pile. "Working alone *at present*." He was talking to himself, not me, though I could hear every word he said.

He shifted some more gear onto the pile. "Shuttle crew kit? Not quite. No charts. No direction finder. No communications gear."

He placed my climbing rope atop the pile. "Ah. Terraformer kit. All there, except the first-aid pouch. Comms in the jalopy. My first guess, if that were all there was.

"Except there is this. Night-vision and infrared monocle. And yet no comms. Recon-scout kit. Silent running. But where is your weapon? Not even a throwing knife."

His gaze darted to mine. "Empty your pockets."

I did as he asked. A couple Trinity-minted pingins, some lint, the data crystal with my contracts on them.

"That's a rather pitiful collection, and not a weapon in there. Must we do a cavity search?"

I stopped leaning against the table and stood to my full height. *You can try.*

His lips twisted into a grin. "I think not, given these additional items not yet cataloged."

He tapped the table. "What is this nonstandard item?"

"Pillowtowel," I said. "I don't like going to bed feeling dirty."

"What a novel experience. You must describe it to me some time."

He began to paw through my most personal items. "A change of underwear and socks. Is that a weapon in the socks? No? A pendant spire, though not made of slaver's chain. Odd material, and odder still that he doesn't wear it, yet he is loath to lose it."

He glanced at me. "A memento from a sweetheart? Remember me always, my errant swain?"

I could feel my jaw working. Just because I have a slow fuse doesn't mean I don't have one.

"Not that, then. A keepsake. A family promise made and kept. Hard to explain to ma and pa if it were to disappear." He nodded to himself. "Something worth fighting for. Very good. I can use that. Is there more to find here?"

He glanced at the table and clapped his hands together. "Oh, look, there is."

"Are you purposely trying to delay me?" I was going to lose my job all because of this Erl buffoon.

"A spare shirt, and what's this wrapped inside? A book. An actual paper book."

"That's private."

"Oh my. Now this is odd. And very rare. Do you know how rare such a book is? It's called a death book, you know. They mostly date from the time of the Exodus."

"I know. Please put it down."

"Does it begin, 'Read me once and I'll make you weep, read me twice and I'll make you wise, read me three times and I'll be forever in your thoughts'?"

"It does not. Now please return my property."

"These books are so perishingly rare, not because they're so ancient, but because they're meant to be burned."

"Please put it down."

"You read them in their entirety thrice, over a span of years, on the anniversary of the author's death. After the third reading you're supposed to torch the original and start your own book. Can you imagine our ancestors, a great asteroid hanging like a hammer in the sky, and they at their quill and anvil, pounding out such a thing, on the hope that one of their children might be chosen for the arks? Knowing that there would soon be nothing left of them but the word-pictures in that book. That even that puny remnant's destiny remained as certain as their own. Ash in the air and a black rain on the tongue."

"I can imagine such a thing. Now please give it back."

"It's recorded that nearly every first-generation survivor followed through on the ritual. The practice died out though, once it began to feel as if there might be a future again. What death books that do remain are largely from these third and fourth generations. Some few early ones do exist though, lost books where the child died before the seventh anniversary of the parent's death. There's a museum on Persephone that pays good money for those."

"I need to get to work. Please return my property and let me go."

"You know there's a way to tell for certain if that's what happened, a death before the seventh year. The reader was expected to jot down their thoughts and understanding after each reading. A number of blank pages are provided in the rear. Such self-confessions increase the value immensely."

The book was only forty pages long, with an illustration on every other page. I didn't want him touching it. I didn't want him reading it. And I didn't want him flipping to the back of it and seeing what I'd written.

"I said that is personal. Give it back."

"Let's see. Yes, it appears this book has only been read through once. Fascinating. Where did you get it?" He flipped through the pages, looking at the pictures.

"From my mother."

"And where did she get it?"

"She wrote it."

"As an experiment? As an homage? How odd. Is she an academic? A historian?" His gaze darted to my face. "A forger?"

"She's dead. Now can I have my stuff back so I can go to work?"

"Oh. I see. I wasn't expecting... I mean that really is extraordinary. Why does it say Academy Muscle on your shirt?"

"It's the name of the company I work for. Or worked for, if this interrogation goes on much longer."

"Yes, but why does it say that in League script, and not in Freeman text?"

"Because we're working in the League Sector?"

"Perhaps." He closed his eyes and tapped his forehead repeatedly.

His eyes snapped open. "And perhaps not."

He shoved the pile of my belongings toward me. "We're

done. Yellow card, free to trade all ports, my good man. Where is this job of yours?"

"Docking ring."

"I'll escort you. It will be faster."

"Okay, but—"

"Will I keep talking?"

"I—"

"Yes, well, you didn't quite say that out loud, did you? I have that effect. You were informed that there is a war on, and that this sector of the station isn't safe at the moment."

"I wasn't. But it doesn't matter. It's safer than starving."

"Yes, well, certainly less drawn out than starving. If at any time you note that we are being stared at, rest assured you are not the center of attention."

"Okay."

"You aren't a very curious person, are you? That was where you ask, 'Oh, is that so?' Or, even better, 'Why is that?'"

"I've got a lot on my mind."

"And it is full."

"What?"

"Your mind. It is out of capacity. Sans headroom, as it were."

"There really are people staring."

"That's because I'm a prisoner of war, and because I'm not usually in uniform. I am well known in the sector, working as I do in the offices of Lord Aster. The hot aspect of the war is newly instantiated, and much disliked, and frankly, shocking to the citizenry. I expect the gunfire will be short-lived though long remembered, and nothing will be settled. A prologue, as it were, to the total war to come."

"Hang on. If you're a prisoner of war, why are you screening entrants? Are the guards prisoners of war also?"

"The guards?"

"The people in the black uniforms checking identification."

"There aren't any people in black uniforms."

"I saw them. I spoke with them."

"A common misconception. The border security agents are regular navy. Their uniforms are thus 'royal navy blue.' Although we may need to come up with another name for the color, as the royal navy is now for all intents and purposes the parliamentary navy."

"The uniforms looked black to me."

"That is because they are actually colored black. But black uniforms aren't allowed under League law. Too many sinister implications. Royal navy blue uniforms have, however, grown darker by the decade so that they are now indistinguishable from black uniforms after a single laundering."

"So is your uniform white?"

"It is gray. As a reservist in the Home Guard, I'm expected to wear the uniform at formal events. Lord Aster is of the opinion that a pan-galactic insurrection is a formal event."

"But if you're a prisoner why were you helping the guards?"

"Because I have it on good authority an attack on Lord Aster's life is imminent. And I was checking entrants in search of his assassin or assassins."

"And you just abandoned your post to escort me to the docking ring?"

"Not at all. The contents of your bag convinced me the assassin is already here, and your comments indicated to me that we should search the docks."

"We? And what do you mean the contents of my bag?"

"I should search, I meant to say. You should proceed to your job and do it as if your life depended on it. What was the date of your mother's death?"

"What?"

"The date."

"Today. Three years ago, standard reckoning. But I don't see—"

"Are you familiar with the iron law of coincidences?"

"I am."

"That would surprise me immeasurably if true. I think it's best we split up here. It wouldn't be profitable to be observed to conspire."

"Conspire?"

"Work together. Coordinate our efforts. Combine our talents. Amplify our individual strengths. One needs both a lever and a place to stand, eh?"

"I'm not conspiring with you or anyone else."

"Charles Newton."

"Who is that?"

"Not who. What. The name you must give when you are arrested."

"Arrested? For what?"

"There is your dock, and there, if I am not mistaken, is the ambulance that was meant for us. You do not need to thank me, but I do hope you rise to the occasion, and prove to be more clever than advertised. Academy Muscle indeed."

"Wait—"

"Of course. Your identity card." He handed me the red card he'd taken from me at the checkpoint.

Someone shouted, and I turned to see who it was, and when I turned back he was gone.

A medical technician shoved past me, and the boss saw me, and started to turn away but changed his mind, and I could see by the gleam in his weasel eyes that he was going to try to use me, or cheat me, or both. There were only the three containers left to unload, and it looked like they'd started on the first one without me. There were a couple of blood trails leading out of the now-open container. A pair of bodies in bright green Academy Muscle shirts were lashed to medical fast-pallets and being loaded into an emergency-response hauler. The bodies weren't moving but the med techs around them seemed busier than they would have been if their patients were dead.

"You're late," the boss said.

I dropped my bug-out kit and dug inside it. I pulled out my hardhands and put them on slowly, one glove at a time. "I was at the meet-up on time."

"Didn't see you," he lied. "Now are you here to work or talk?"

"Work."

We marched anti-spinward to where the next of the unopened FFEs lay welded to the ring. One of my coworkers was already there and waiting, the man, which didn't surprise me. Of the four of us he was the laziest, and it figured if anyone got hurt on the job it wouldn't be him, just based on the amount of hours spent actually doing work. I asked the boss what happened back there, when they opened the other FFE.

"There was something alive in there. Things were fine at first, but then the girls shifted some boxes and suddenly it's like a whirlwind of blood and screams. Somebody called the emergency service and they showed up right before you got here."

"After you rescued the women from the container."

"The emergency crew got them out."

"You *left them* in there?"

"I had to keep whatever was in there from getting loose on the station."

"You *locked them* in there?"

"The hatch is open now."

"You warned the emergency crew about the thing inside. And they got rid of it."

"Sure. Look, what's done is done. I got the codes for these last two, and once we unload these we're out of here, and you'll get paid. In full."

I watched the medics pile into their hauler and pull away, heading toward what I imagined was the hospital, unless it was the morgue.

I stood well back from the FFE and so did the boss this time.

He spoke to my coworker in the language they used amongst themselves, the guy punched on the FFE's control panel for a while, and then there was a loud click. The FFE hatch began to open and there was a hissing noise, like an air leak, then the hatch snapped open and the guy was gone.

I reached out and grabbed the boss as he was being sucked out, and I nearly missed.

Emergency depressurization alarms were sounding, blast doors were slamming closed, and this part of the ring was isolated. Then there was some sort of viscous liquid leaking out of the overhead, and the liquid dripped on the deck, expanded, and began to harden. It was the stuff they called fast patch, and as it expanded and skinned over, it began to slap into the ring on either side of the container opening, then slap into itself as it was drawn toward vacuum. Next it started to fuse solid, and that went on for a while until the pressure on my ears changed and it looked like the breach was sealed.

I still had my one arm wrapped around a big deck to deck-head conduit and my other arm stretched out, the boss's wrist in that hand. My jaw was still flapped open, because the whole process happened so fast, life to death in an eye blink. That's what these space-born people lived with every day.

He glanced at my hand, and the field-reinforced glove encasing it, and he could see that it was powered up and wrapped around his dominant arm. He got this sickly look on his face, a look that he hadn't had a second before, when all he thought had changed was that one of his lackeys had been sucked into space.

We were right underneath one of the alarm klaxons, and every time it sounded loose scales of hardened fast patch danced on the deck.

"That one's empty," I shouted. "Let's go see what's in the last one."

"Yeah," he shouted back. "Let's do that."

The depressurization alarms were still screaming as we faced the last of the unopened FFEs.

I tapped the boss's shoulder and pointed at the control panel and shouted. "You drive!"

The alarm cut off suddenly and it was like I was shouting at him, not to be heard, but like a threat.

He looked at me and grinned. "I don't think you understand the situation here, big boy."

A man stepped from the shadows. "He has a lot on his mind at the moment."

"Me too," the boss said. "You're late."

"Fashionably so. What have you found?"

The man was dressed in a skinsuit and wearing hardhands. He held a rebreather in one hand and a small wrapped package in the other, one not much larger than two hands held side by side, and flat, like a plate. The last time I'd seen him he'd been dressed in a gray uniform.

"There's nothing here," the boss said.

"That is a pity." The man glanced at me. "Is he telling the truth?"

"How would I know? They never told me what they were looking for."

"Didn't they?"

"Why would we? He's just muscle."

"There's been a change in plans," the man said. He shoved the package into my hands. "Give that to the first weeping woman you meet."

"He'll talk," the boss said. "We agreed. No loose ends."

"Well, there's bound to be at least one loose end, isn't there?" He turned his attention to me, and I saw it again, the wolf behind his eyes. "You've cost me a great deal of revision, my good man. I hope you prove worth it. Now go into the remaining container and close the hatch behind you. "

The boss laughed. "Just follow the blood trails."

"You'd best go now," the man said.

"Hand me a rebreather and let's get out of here," the boss said.

"Yes, about that." The man stepped toward the FFE's control panel and began punching in numbers. "As I explained, there's been a change of plans."

I didn't hear the rest, because by then I was sprinting toward the open container. I knew what was going to happen next because I'd already seen it happen once.

I was reaching for the hatch controls when the pressure on the docking ring changed. I slammed the hatch closed, heard it dog, and then I was in the dark, and the booming pulses of the depressurization klaxons were hammering against the other side of the hatch. I slumped against the hatch and let myself slide down.

My heart was trying to bang itself out of my ribcage. My eyeballs burned. The smell of blood clung to the air, the deck sticky beneath my palms. I figured it would be a while before they sealed the breach and they thought to search the other containers, and then they'd get me out.

I was wondering how long that would be when something brushed my leg and growled.

I slid slowly back up the wall, so I could reach the control panel. I eased the lighting controls up.

A jumble of boxes, piled haphazardly to the ceiling and blood spattered. A dried slick of blood, two dried slicks, crusty at the edges, but still tacky. And in the tacky bits, paw prints. Not the biggest paw prints I'd ever seen but big enough, and plenty of evidence that whatever was walking around on them wasn't to be messed with.

The depressurization klaxons banged on outside. It seemed like they were going on far longer than they had the first time.

I tried to peer into the jumble of boxes and I couldn't see anything. Plenty of places to hide. Places I could stick my hand into and feel around in if I ever grew tired of having two hands.

I checked the environmental controls on the FFE. It had atmosphere. It had light. It had heat. It would run out of air in twenty hours unless it could get some from outside. They could patch the leak and air up this part of the dock in twenty hours, right? Unless they didn't think they needed to, since there wouldn't be any life signs showing in this section of the ring. They could just leave it airless until someone decided to follow through on those redevelopment plans the boss had mentioned.

*First things first.* I was trapped in a box with something that could maim or murder me any minute. And I might run out of air in twenty hours. Or someone might decide to open the space-side doors to retrieve their cargo and I'd be sucked out into vacuum. All three were important. Only one was urgent. And that was the only one I knew how to do something about.

All this time I'd been thinking that there wasn't anything I could do on a space station that couldn't be done better by someone born there.

All this time I'd been wrong.

I placed my bug-out bag gently on the deck and pulled out a couple ration bars and a liter of water. I drank the water down to the halfway point. I still had on my gloves from earlier, so I concentrated, and adjusted the field so that it extended a centimeter beyond the tip of my right index finger. I sharpened it with a gesture and ran it around the liter bottle. The top of the bottle fell off and rolled across the deck.

I peeled the rations out of their wrappers. Then, moving very slowly, I walked within two paces of the jumble of boxes and placed my improvised water bowl and food supply on the deck. Then I went back to the far end of the compartment and dug out my spotting monocle and my portable shovel.

And I waited.

I've never really enjoyed the killing part of hunting. The waiting part I liked a lot. If there was a pest around the farm and the sensors didn't pick it up clearly, my dad would ask us all to sit up and watch for it. My brothers found it boring but I'd gotten in the habit of doing two things at once. I could think about something totally unrelated while I waited. And whenever what I was waiting for showed up, I could stop instantly and focus on the matter at hand. Once we knew what it was that was spooking the donkeys or eating the chickens we could come up with a plan to do something about it. Most of the time that still involved killing, but not every time.

In this case?

I didn't know.

I picked up my portable shovel and flicked the handle to full extension. I fired it up and it was dead silent. If the man in the gray uniform hadn't messed with it, I wouldn't have dared turn it on for fear of spooking whatever was hiding in the pile of boxes. As it was I ran through the presets to the smallest and pointiest shovel configuration, a trencher that would cut through the densest mat of roots. Then I touched both the up and down controls at the same time and held them, and the shovel kept getting narrower, and pointier, the field more concentrated and the edge more refined.

Then I powered it off and went back to waiting. The shovel would remember that setting when next I turned it on.

After a long while I spotted movement. It was almost like watching an empty collar dragging a bloodstained chain, so well did the creature blend in with its background. It was only after it had sniffed the water, and dipped a paw in to drink, that its camouflage dropped for an instant and I could see it in its natural colors.

It was a mong hu, but a young one. I couldn't tell how long the chain was, but from the blood spatter to either side of me I'd say long enough for it to reach me anywhere in the container.

Its orange fur was matted beneath the collar, and bloodied, and in places bare skin shown through, raw and swollen. It dipped water daintily from the improvised bowl with its paw, and licked the water from there, and when it saw me watching, stopped.

Its paws were huge for its size, and its ears as well. It had a long tail that might well have resembled a plume if its fur hadn't been blood-slicked to its skin and matted. Its eyes were dull copper and its chin white, excepting in spots, where blisters like acne shown through the fur. The white fur continued down it neck, and where I'd first thought it was entirely orange I could now see that there was a white swirl on its side.

A kitten, I decided, though larger than the largest barn cat I'd ever seen. Bigger than a lynx, smaller than a panther. Lots of claws and fangs, usually deadly. An adult mong hu could grow to three times my mass and all of it rippling muscle and pent-up aggression. Mong hu were rare, and outside of a seanscéal, I'd only read about them. Everything I knew said the same things. Don't surprise them, and whatever you do, don't make them angry.

It watched me, and when I didn't do anything, went back to drinking.

Mong hu were genetically engineered cats. But they were more than that to Freemen. Not just space-born Freemen, but all of us. We'd grown apart as families do, but there was a time when all Freemen were one, and alone, and slaves, and if not for the mong hu we might yet be. The mong hu seanscéal was a long and popular one, even though it was also told in school, every year, on the first day of class, and the last. Mong hu weren't pets and they weren't property. They were allies, and kin, respected comrades-in-arms, revered for their sacrifice and their steadfastness. We had a deal with the mong hu. A contract. The first contract, and the pattern for every contract since.

I watched that kitten drink and thought hard. If my old da were to walk in and see what I was looking at there would be two wars on the station. And while the League seemed to consider war a pastime, our folk looked on it as a waste, and a last resort. War was what we did when someone had gone past talking to, and earned a killing.

When the kitten finished drinking it moved on to the ration bars. It sniffed them, and eyeballed me, and began to test its food. I could see that its whole belly was white and that it had white swirls on both sides. I could also see its ribs beneath its dull coat, and I figured it had been chained up without water and food for days.

It watched me and growled while it ate. It managed to eat both ration bars. I peeled a couple more out of their wrappers and tossed them toward it. It watched them land, crept over to them, and sniffed them, and then ignored them.

It went to a corner beside the boxes and began to take a bath. After a while its eyes drooped and it began to purr. A while later the purring stopped and it curled up into a ball, a paw over its eyes.

I figured now was the time. I picked up my portable shovel and flicked it to full extension. I powered the shovel up and a bright-blue spear sprouted on the business end of the shaft.

I padded over to the kitten as silently as I could and squared up to the job. A half measure wouldn't do. The kitten's eye blinked open and it saw me, shovel raised high.

I stabbed the shovel down, burying the blade a centimeter into the deck.

The chain parted cleanly.

The kitten began to purr.

I ate one of the ration bars.

Then I put the second ration bar beside another improvised bowl of water.

"I die free," I whispered, which was the famous last line of the mong hu seanscéal.

I'd thought that story was about slavery as a kid, but lately I'd begun to think it was about courage. Now I wasn't sure. I thought that maybe it wasn't about anything so simple.

If I'd gone to sleep and woke up dead it wouldn't have been worse than waking up knowing I'd left that kitten chained the whole night through. We're no better or worse than the choices we make. Or don't make.

I slept for a while, and woke, and the kitten was eating. I peeled and tossed my last ration bar and went back to sleep.

When I woke again I was on my back, and the kitten was standing on my chest. It growled and I could see that it really did have fangs that gleamed like diamond, just like in the seanscéal.

I balled my hands into fists and my hardhands powered up, and I told it, "Don't kill me yet."

I grabbed both sides of that collar and yanked.

The kitten nearly nipped me when I tossed the collar aside and it clanked. But it changed its mind at the last minute, and I let my breath out real slow.

"The power of ten squared," I told the kitten.

It hopped off me and began rooting around in my bug-out kit.

I began digging through the jumble of boxes in the container and I did find something else that didn't belong there —besides the kitten, and my own self, of course.

Later that night I read my mother's death book for the second time. When I was done I didn't feel any wiser. It was a made-up story. It wasn't about her, or me, or us, together.

In the morning an emergency crew opened the container,

and I walked out without a sleeping bag and half tent but with a kitten curled up and sleeping in my bug-out bag.

I made it all the way to the sector border before they detained me.

I handed over my red identification card and the guard glanced at it briefly, then he looked at it closely, then he held it up next to my face and handed it back and said, "Have a nice day."

And then I was through the border, and back under Freeman custom and contract. I was still wearing my Academy Muscle shirt, but it was a little worse for wear. I spotted a woman in her prime and a girl a few years younger than me. They were both wearing torn and bloodstained Academy Muscle shirts over what looked like League paramedic uniforms. The woman was crying. The girl was not.

I handed the woman the package. I hadn't opened it, but I knew what was in it. You can't carry a death book for a span of years without recognizing its weight. When she felt the package in her hands, she knew what it was too. She started crying harder.

The girl motioned for me to bend down, and I thought it was because she wanted to tell me something she didn't want other people to hear. When I stooped to listen, her hand snaked out, and she grabbed my collar and yanked.

I jerked upright, and she stood beaming at a piece of cloth in her hand. The laundry tag off my shirt.

"It's true," she said. "You people write your names on your clothing, so when it's stolen you can hunt down the thief and make them pay."

"Is that what you think?" Because it was sort of true, only she'd gotten it backward. We wrote our names on our clothing so we wouldn't accidentally steal someone else's, and they'd have to hunt us down and make us pay.

"What I think," she said, "is that if I'd asked your name you would have lied to me. And now you won't need to." She glanced at the scrap of cloth in her hand. Then she stared at my face like she was an orbital drone mapping a continent that shouldn't be there. "See you later, Mr. Muscle."

And that's all I have to say about the second time.

Except that I found out later that the weeping woman was Lady Tabatha Aster, and the precocious girl her daughter, Lady Sarah Aster, and that the pair of them were being held captive and used against Lady Tabatha's husband, Lord Merlin Aster, who was on the station at the time and caught up in the short war that year.

My two female coworkers hadn't made it off the docking ring alive, but dressed in their by-now-familiar green shirts and carrying forged identities, the ladies Aster had escaped to the Freeman sector, and were waiting for Lord Aster to join them. He didn't, and when she saw me come through the security gate Lady Tabatha knew he hadn't made it out. And handing her the death book just confirmed that.

I never did learn who the boss was, or my coworkers, though I believe I would recognize the language they spoke amongst themselves if I were to hear it again.

As for the officer in gray, I was told that was Lord Aster himself, as the Queen's merlin is listed as killed on the docks at Trinity Station, in a tragic cargo-handling accident on that day.

I'm not sure I believe any of that. Neither that he was Lord Aster, nor that Lord Aster died on the docks on the anniversary of my mother's death.

As to what I found that didn't belong there, it wasn't much. Just this data crystal. One unlike any I'd ever seen.

I think that was what they were looking for. The whole container was filled with junk from a pet store and this was the only thing that stood out, other than a dead mouse in a cage that stunk like it had been dead a week. It sounds crazy but I got so busy with school and trying to fit in that I forgot all about the crystal until yesterday. Now I can't get it out of my mind.

I was a kid, fresh off the shuttle back then, with no context. Now I've glimpsed the edge of the wider world, and I think that there was a lot going on there that I didn't understand.

And that this crystal may be a lot more important than I imagined.

CIARÁN STARED at the work table's surface for a while before he glanced up at the luminaire overhead and spoke. "Can you read the crystal?"

"Leave it and I will try."

"Now do you believe me? Everyone else pays, but I come away with a friend on the station, and not just any friend, but a friend straight out of a storybook. Suddenly I'm like a deck-striding merchant captain, with a mong hu at my side, and I haven't even attended a single Academy class yet.

"It all got easier after that, tough but bearable, and worth it, because I wasn't just doing it for myself anymore. I had an ally. A partner. And I had to do well, because the only way we deserved to stay together was if I graduated and earned a slot on an interstellar. And here we are, Wisp and I. Together still."

The ship's minder was much more experienced than he was, and expressly designed to carry out its mission. But so were the boss and his crew, and that hadn't worked out well for them. Ciarán wanted to avoid the same mistake, and the only way that could happen was if the ship's minder saw him as someone whose opinion was worth considering, not as a substitute for its own judgement, but as a valuable addition to its understanding.

"Show me this death book."

*Everything valuable comes with a price.*

"I will. Tomorrow, when I read it for the third time."

"Show it to me now."

"We'll read it together at midnight. It's not that long to wait."

The ship's minder said nothing.

"Well?"

"Not a minute later."

"Count on it."

The overhead luminaire dropped to the table. It picked up the data crystal and scuttled away on eight spidery limbs.

"I guess we're done here," Ciarán said.

*Until midnight.*

## 6

_____

Two empty hours later he revised his thought. *Nearly done here.* He'd thought it over and decided. There was yet one task awaiting, and it was better done the day *before* than the day *of* obligation.

Ciarán shifted in his seat and toggled the workstation awake.

He opened his message queue and found the offending transmission.

The merchant captain had believed the contents of this message would cause him to not just abandon the mission, and break his word, but breach his contract as well. Breaching his contract would mean he would be abandoning Wisp, who was bound to the merchant captain by the big cat's own contract, a contract he'd agreed to for her in error, his first mistake as a merchant apprentice but certainly not his last.

He couldn't imagine anything that could make him breach that contract now, any more than he could imaging renouncing the Oath.

But at Ambidex, or before?

Maybe.

Aoife nic Cartaí hadn't known him very well back then, and he'd thought the ship insane and its crew pirates.

He hadn't known himself very well, either. He still didn't, but he knew himself better, and he knew what was at stake, and it wasn't simply a life of adventure and profit amongst the stars.

Ciarán took a deep breath.

And opened the message.

---

## 7

Lorelei Ellis stood in front of a low stone stable. That building wouldn't draw an eye on the mainland but was the third largest manmade structure on Oileán Chléire. She'd clearly been riding, and had a fine stallion's reins in her hand. Yet she wasn't dressed for riding at all, but rather wore an outfit as black and matte in sheen as *Quite Possibly Alien*'s hull.

She had changed, physically at least, and now appeared everything Ciarán's brother Niall had said, and more.

"I promised myself I wouldn't contact you," she said. "But I promised your mother I would, and a promise to another trumps a promise to one's self."

She scrubbed a toe through the dust. The horse began to tug on the reins and she let it go. It began to graze at the verge of the long gravel drive that lead up from the little cove below the original Ellis homestead.

"My father's dead, as if you haven't figured that out from these hideous weeds I'm obliged to wear. The coroner's declared the death an accident." She gazed straight into the recording device. "That's not what I wanted to say, but this.

That I was down to our boggy acre today, and there was a man, and he was asking after the owner. Said he would pay up big if I knew how to reach him. I don't think he knew I was the lease holder, as the lease was in my old da's name, and I didn't give him mine."

She smiled to herself, as if she'd thought up a joke, and it hadn't made it to her lips yet.

"He's a blow-in, and staying with the Gant, but that isn't the half of it. I heard he's making offers all around, cash money, though I imagine the Gant has warned him away from your da, so it's unlikely you'd hear about this directly.

"I've spoken to the Diarmuid, and he said to say hello, and that if you were to hear that he's turned up dead, don't for a minute believe it was an accident, or even true. There's no reason to come home on his account, and you're a fool if you do. Your brothers are on high alert, and capable men, and you're neither wanted nor needed. That is a direct quote."

She pointed a finger at the recording device. "You're not to be worried on my account, either. But on to the point.

"I swore to your mother I'd keep an eye on the lake in the sky for her, and I have, and that's why I'm recording this today. Someone's been flying drones up there, and mapping the whole of the mountain. I don't know if it's this same Commodore Olek who's staying with the local gombeen man, but I imagine it is. And now I've kept my word, to another, at least, and I'll leave you to your journeying.

"I won't say I miss you, because everywhere I look I see you."

She smiled a little, and gazed at the recorder with eyes the precise shade of willow bark.

"I will say that having a definitive article in my name isn't the joy it used to be."

She kicked a clod of dirt and gazed up at the sky before returning her gaze to the recorder.

"I will see you when I see you, Ciarán mac Diarmuid."

The display went black.

He closed the message queue.

He powered the workstation down.

He needed to think. Laura didn't just know how to press his buttons. She knew how to play him like a squeezebox. Commodore Olek on Oileán Chléire? She couldn't have known that to make it up. And she didn't make things up. The truth was enough to knot his guts. She hadn't needed him. She would be stronger, and happier, and more herself without him around.

What did this message change?

Anything?

Everything?

*He should have deleted it unopened.*

Someone knocked on the merchant's day-cabin hatch.

Ciarán levered himself out of his seat and went to see what fresh new terror awaited.

# 8

---

"I thought you had an open-door policy." Maura Kavanagh was dressed in her best utilities, as if she was ready and waiting for the liberty boat. She wasn't glittered up but nicely turned out, so maybe not the liberty boat, but an away mission, one where being taken seriously mattered. She wore the pendant spire and it looked good on her, but then everything looked good on her, and she knew it. He wracked his brain for the last time he'd seen her done up like a First Families daughter, and couldn't recall a single instance.

Ciarán glanced toward the bridge. "What's wrong?" She was meant to be on duty.

"You are. Why aren't you ready?"

"Ready for what?"

"Agnes's announcement."

"Announcement about what?"

"How would I know? She sent a message earlier, that we were all to meet on the bridge in formal dress. She had something she wanted to say and all of us there to hear it."

"Hear it when?"

"Now."

"Tell her I didn't get the message. I'll be there in ten."

# 9

Ciarán and Wisp were the last to arrive, joining the remainder of the crew standing along the aft bulkhead, where the vessel's name, date of commissioning, and first port of registration stood out stark and uncompromising in the half-light, an odd mix of the archaic loops and swirls of second-epoch League script and the jagged slashes of the Freeman text overlaying them.

Ko Shan had taken her usual station at sensors, although without the full immersion rig and goop. Maura Kavanagh rested behind the navigator's station. Medic Watanabe had taken a seat at the piloting station normally occupied by Helen Konstantine, carefully avoiding the array of controls as if they were yet live. Today her gilded environmental mask wore the placid face of a sleeping mong hu.

Mrs. Amati and Engineer Hess were dressed in their League major's and warrant officer's uniforms respectively, and even Mr. Gagenot wore not just the night-blue utilities of the ship's victualer, but the pendant spire.

"Glad we dressed for the occasion," Ciarán whispered to Wisp, who swished her freshly combed tail once before taking a seat. He'd taken to wearing the spire prior to his first trip down to Gallarus Surface, and it was now a regular part of his daily attire. His utilities were freshly laundered, and other than the addition of a merchant-in-charge pip on his collar, he might have passed for the same raw merchant apprentice who'd stepped aboard *Quite Possibly Alien* less than a year before.

"Ship," the ship's captain said.

"I am here." The ship's alto voice seemed to come from everywhere and nowhere.

"Sxipestro," the ship's captain said.

"I am here," a voice inside Ciarán's head replied. Not for the first time he wondered if all of the ship's crew perceived the minder as he did, or if its tone and inflection varied by the hearer.

"I've asked all of you here to make an announcement and to act as witnesses. As some of you know, tomorrow is an auspicious day in the Hundred Planets, as it marks the turning of the Celestial Clock."

"The what?" Hess said.

"The day of ascendence for the Eng," Ko Shan said. "When the Emperor's mandate passed from the naturally born to his *engineered* descendants."

"Not merely the Emperor's mandate, but the civilian authority of the Ojin and Alexandrian governments as well," Natsuko said.

"Splinter groups," Swan said. "One presumes they no longer celebrate this anniversary."

"The Huangxu do not celebrate it," Ko Shan said. "With all due respect, Ship's Captain, only the Huangxu Eng revere death as birth."

"We do not revere death," Swan said. "We celebrate our forbearers' defiance of it. We reaffirm their decision to sacrifice their authority to see that their children survived. But that is beside the point, and not what I wish to discuss."

"Hang on," Ciarán said. "You're saying tomorrow is a particularly important day to you and all the Huangxu Eng?"

"To all the surviving children of Earth," Swan said.

"It's the anniversary of the planetary asteroid strike," Ko Shan said. "As recorded by the Unified Empire prior to the Great Schism."

"Not merely by the Empire. As recorded by all who survived," Swan said. "We remember. And because we remember, decisions of import are often made on that day. That is why I asked you all to join me here, to witness my defiance of convention. Ko Shan, please display the message."

The same message Ciarán had reviewed with the ship's captain appeared on all of the bridge displays. The imbedded images appeared incredibly sharp.

"Ugh, that guy," Maura Kavanagh said. "It's about time someone arrested him."

"I beg your pardon?" the ship's captain said.

"She's referring to the other man in cuffs, Agnes," Mrs. Amati said. "Not Captain Swan."

"The Huangxu Eng prisoner is your brother?" Maura said. "Danny Swan of Truxton's *Rose*? Last time I saw him he had two ears."

"As he did last I saw him," the ship's captain said. "Who is this other captive?"

"Trouble," Maura said. "Claims to be a history professor at the Home Guard Academy on Cordame. Hector something. Very informed on second-epoch stuff. Aoife and I met with him before going to Murrisk. She blames him in part for what happened afterward. He's a talker, and bent as they come. One or the other in a coconspirator is bearable, but not both."

Swan seemed to have lost her train of thought. She stared at the display in silence.

"I've met that man," Ciarán said.

"And?" Amati said.

"Look closely at the image. And at his hands."

"They're glowing blue," Natsuko said.

"What does this mean?" Swan said.

*It means no prison can hold him.* "I'd like to show the crew another message that may be related," Ciarán said. "Ko Shan, can you access the ship's general account?"

"I can," Ko Shan said. "And I have. Is it the message you've tagged?"

"It is."

A message header flashed across the bridge displays before the displays flashed black, and then the message content began.

The image stream appeared to have been captured from an overhead drone. A spreading three-story residence monopolized the distant view, arcs of tall trees framing the structure and a sculpture park before it, artwork seemingly gathered from across the League flanking a curving paved drive. In the foreground a trio of people hiked along the drive as it bisected a manicured lawn. Nearly dusk, the shadows of the statuary stretched long, and the shadows of the walkers as well. Wind noise in the audio stream rose and fell, and with it a distant low humming, like bees in a hive.

The drone centered it sensors on the walkers and dove toward them. It hovered several meters above them. There were two women, one on either side of a man, each assisting the man, his arms draped over their shoulders. They seemed to be holding the man upright, although his legs appeared to move under their own power.

"Is it one of ours?" the taller woman said.

The shorter woman touched a device in her hands and said, "It is now. But we'll have to talk fast."

She gazed up at the drone, and it focused on her face. A series of facial recognition boxes began to flash across the display but couldn't seem to establish a lock.

She was in her late teens, early twenties. She gazed up at the drone and grinned.

"Charles Newton, you are a hard man to find. I am in need of some muscle and wondered if we might meet up, either at your place or mine."

She glanced over her shoulder, where the buzzing had increased, and the drone's sensors followed her gaze. A black cloud had engulfed the building in the distance, and what looked like lighting flashed in the cloud, but red lightning. The drone's audio sensors began to pick up the sounds of plasma fire. Ordinary fires began to break out inside the cloud and black smoke began to pour into the sky, until something volatile ignited, and the video and audio sensors overloaded; when they recovered, the man and the taller women were trying to clamor to their feet and the shorter woman cursed, stared up at the drone, and said. "Your place, it is, then."

She pointed a needler at the drone. "See you soon, Mr. Muscle."

The feed went blank.

"I'm out of here," Hess said. He headed for the hatch.

Amati blocked his exit. "Hold up." She caught Ciarán's attention. "Hess and I received messages today. Konstantine as well, though I'm not certain she's seen hers yet."

"You've been recalled to active duty," Ciarán said.

"Not hardly," Hess said. "We've been cashiered. Told to turn in our kit at the first League port we hit. Said maybe Aster's Army would have us, but the regular navy was done with us."

"Wow, that's raw," Maura said. "But run it back, Ko Shan, and look at the display."

Ko Shan looped the replay so that the building seemed to be enveloped by a black cloud and destroyed, over and over again.

Maura pointed at the display. "What *is* that?"

"That *was* Sunbury Park, on Columbia Surface," Amati

said. "And that is what the decapitation of the League's Domestic Intelligence Service looks like."

"Not what I asked," Maura said. "I mean what is the *weapon.*"

"No idea," Amati said. "Something new."

Ko Shan broke the loop and froze the replay. "Does anyone recognize these people?"

"The man is Lord Aster," Amati said. "The Queen's merlin."

"I'd heard the League's spymaster was dead," Ko Shan said.

Amati stared at the frozen display. "He might be by now."

Ko Shan froze the display on a clear frame showing all three faces. "And the women?"

"Lady Tabatha Aster and her daughter, Lady Sarah Aster," Ciarán said.

Amati stared at him. The entire crew stared at him.

"We're acquainted," Ciarán said.

"How?" Amati said.

"He can't tell you," Maura said. "Being a stickler for custom. You're not just asking about his own past, but someone else's."

Ciarán nodded.

"The trick is in the asking," Maura said. "Do either of them have any distinguishing moles or tattoos that aren't visible in public?"

Ciarán felt his face heat. "How would I know?"

"Well, do you have anything that was once theirs, or they have anything that was once yours?"

"I doubt it."

"But you might."

"I think I'd know."

"But they might."

"I wouldn't know for certain."

"Is it the mother has it?"

"Maura, this isn't funny," Ciarán said.

"Is it the daughter has it?"

"Enough," Ciarán said.

"He has an arm's-length relationship with Lady Tabatha," Maura said. "And he's been close enough to Lady Sarah for her to pick his pocket. Or he hers."

"Why would you know any of that lot?" Hess said. "They're poison."

"I don't *know* them," Ciarán said. "I said we're acquainted. I met them on Trinity Station. It seemed entirely coincidental at the time. The man in that image claimed to work for Lord Aster. I'd never heard the name until that moment. He was wearing a Home Guard major's uniform when I met him, though I'd not been aware of the affiliation and rank at the time."

"Are you also acquainted with this Lord Aster?" Natsuko said.

Ciarán felt his ears burn. "I thought that man might be Lord Aster. He gave me this." He pulled a card from his pocket and handed it to Ko Shan. "Please pass that to Mrs. Amati."

"Look at that," Maura said. "His merchant's license has turned as red as his ears."

"It's not a merchant's license," Amati said. "It's a League-registered alien ID."

"Whose?" Hess said.

Ko Shan glanced at the card. "Charles Newton's."

Hess snatched the card from Ko Shan's fingers. "Let's get a look at this pinhole."

Amati leaned on his shoulder. Her gaze never left Ciarán's. "Let's."

Hess glanced at Ciarán. He glanced at the card. He glanced at Ciarán. "Explain this."

"I can't," Ciarán said. "I don't understand it."

"This Hector fellow isn't Lord Aster," Amati said. "And Ciarán isn't Charles Newton."

"And you know this because?" Hess said.

"Because," Amati said, "the man being carried away from Sunbury Park is Lord Aster. And because Charles Newton isn't a man. He's a myth."

"And this Hector the Home Guard major?" Natsuko said.

"I'll ask around," Amati said. "Once we're back in a system with a superluminal node."

The ship's captain cleared her throat.

"If you recall," Swan said, "I have something I wish to say."

Ciarán scrubbed his palm across his face and nodded. "Say it."

*How much worse could things get?*

"My life is my own. As I will not live as slave to any man's will, I will not ask any man to live as slave to mine."

"That's the Freeman Oath," Ciarán said.

"I know that," Agnes Swan said.

"You're taking the Oath," Ciarán said.

"I just did, Freeman whelp. And I've signed up for the merchant's examination. I expect to complete it before you."

"Two merchants on the same vessel," Maura said. "Three if you count Aoife. We'll have to outfit a compartment as a Guild Hall."

"Two merchants and a merchant's apprentice," Swan said. "Unless the merchant apprentice is needed elsewhere."

The ship's clock struck midnight.

"He is." Ciarán strode from the compartment.

## 10

Ciarán mac Diarmuid paced the merchant's day cabin. The hour of midnight was entirely symbolic on a starship. *Quite Possibly Alien*, like most superluminal vessels, used League standard time, which wasn't synchronized with Columbia system time, as was often thought, but with a constellation of reference clocks said to have been assembled on Earth over six thousand "standard" years ago.

"Sxipestro," he said.

"I am here."

Ciarán placed the death book on the work table. "Can you see the book?"

The light fixture overhead shifted minutely. "I can. Clearly."

"Good." The ship's minder wasn't impervious to persuasion. Since Ciarán had been on board and speaking with it nightly, its language had altered. It used to answer yes and no, like the Erl did. Tonight it spoke in affirmations and negations as if it had been born to the spire.

"This is the object I spoke of. It isn't just a story in words, like the ones I've related to you, but a story and pictures. I find the illustrations most disturbing."

"Because?"

"Because I don't think my mother could have made them. Not the woman I knew, anyway. I understand they are in the style of Blake Christian, an artist popular in ancient times."

"Popular, and an imposter," the ship's minder said. "His work consisted of found art, a cache of prediaspora manuscripts discovered and passed off as his own."

"Do you think that is pertinent?"

"I don't know. Let's see the work."

"First, I need to explain that this is a story. It didn't really happen. The people in the story aren't real. It isn't a memoir, or an account of events, but something entirely invented by a woman slowly losing her mind. She wrote four of these death books and the three she wrote for my brothers are normal. Recollections of her life on the farm. Stories about family life she wanted them to remember. Wishes for their futures. A final farewell.

"I haven't read theirs. The book is private for the person who receives it, perhaps the most private item one can possess short of a love letter from one's beloved. But I asked about their books, and they told me. Theirs were standard printouts with still images of family and life on the farm.

"Mine is written in longhand, with color illustrations that... Well, you'll see. Also, I think she died before she could finish it. The story just... stops."

"Is that all?"

"That's all I remember about it. I haven't looked at it in three years. A lot has changed in my life. It feels like I'm reading it with new eyes."

"And you find this disconcerting."

"I find it terrifying. Like I said, a lot of coincidences happen around the time I read this."

Ciarán turned to the first page. "Whenever you are ready."

"I am ready. Begin."

Ciarán flipped the death book open.
And began.

# 11

The Willow Bride's Curse
by Cassandra mac Diarmuid (née Poole)

R ead me once and I will make you cry. Read me twice and I will make you wise. Read me three times and you'll never be rid of me.

ONCE UPON A TIME there was a farmer and he had four sons, each of them stronger, and smarter, and more handsome than the next, all but the one son, who wasn't any of those things.

"Not yet he isn't," the farmer would tell his neighbors, and the farmer's wife would look at the man she'd wed, and shake her head in sorrow, because she knew something the farmer didn't know about his own son.

The boy was cursed, and the curse all her fault.

She didn't speak a word of this, then or later, but carried her burden in silence so that it grew to be a stone in her breast when she gazed upon the boy. At night, while she lay in her sleeping, she dreamed, and as often as not, woke to find her cheeks moist, and her heart beating like a moth's wings from the fretting over the strange boy, and the hope of his future. For he was a strange boy, no doubt. Moody, and silent, and solitary. She had made him that way, on purpose. She had made him fit for a sacrifice.

Now this farm was in a long, narrow valley between the hills, with steeply wooded slopes, and high pasture for grazing, and through its heart a bubbling stream splashed over rocks, and settled in deep pools, and raced between grassy banks beneath the willows, all the way from the mountains to the sea.

A strong party of men, well equipped, might follow that stream to its source in a week, given the weather cooperated, and assuming they showed the proper deference to the land, and the creatures of the land, and every living thing beneath the sky and beneath the ground, and between the banks of the stream they called the Willow Bride's Tears.

The stream ran swiftly downslope from a crater lake too small to name on maps or charts, but which locals called the Source, and it was to there her thoughts returned again and again. The ground up there was too steep and boulder strewn to land a flyer, and the winds too unpredictable, so that the only way up or down was on foot for the last four days, and for the first three, foot or ass, or mule.

If arriving at the Source was a work in itself, returning was a dozen times harder, as downhill every stone turned underfoot, and the weather seldom held for more than a day at a time, and few were lucky enough to traipse across such a great wild landscape without running afoul of wolves of the country, or hungering after a salmon of the stream, or lusting after the gems of the earth. The wolves were dense as trees on the hillside, and the salmon would jump onto the spit to tempt a man.

And the gems? They were big as duck eggs and scattered on the ground like hailstones after a summer storm.

That's what people said. But that wasn't all they said.

They said the steep hills, and the swift mountain stream, and the deep icy lake at its source were the private demesne of the Willow Bride. A great dragon slumbered beneath the lake and would wake at her command. Taking so much as a salmon scale from her waters, or a pebble from her lake's icy shore, would rain doom upon the trespasser, and that doom would follow them down the mountain, and over the sea, and across the trackless void between the stars. Such was the power of her wrath that even time itself could not shackle it, or her, for the Willow Bride was Folk, and the Folk had followed the People across the stars, though no one living knew how, or knowing, would say.

One day the farmer's wife was in the kitchen, and she was after drawing a big pot of water for the boiling, and she glanced down at the watery surface and found the Willow Bride staring back. She dropped the pot, and cracked the floor tiles, and soaked her apron to her knees, and her knees buckled, and she reached for the back of a chair, and missed, and kept falling, and then all was black, and she knew in an instant she was beneath the ground, and beneath the lake, and in the cold, and almost silence, but for the rumbling snore of the Willow Bride's dragon.

"You have stolen from me," the Willow Bride said, and the farmer's wife denied it, but she knew the Willow Bride spoke truth. All those years loving the farmer, and raising his sons, and building a life were lived in the shadow of the mountain. Every drop of water she'd swallowed was a theft of the Willow Bride's tears, and every drop her sons had swallowed, and the man she loved as well.

"What do you want from me?" the farmer's wife said.

"What is mine."

"I can't give you that," the farmer's wife said, because she knew what the Willow Bride wanted, and that was her sons.

"One will do," the Willow Bride said, and in that instant the farmer's wife admitted to herself that she had planned for this day, from the birth of her second son, and prayed it would never come, but now that it had the fact of her betrayal struck her like a flail, and she saw how that self-knowledge would murder her a little each day. But the cost seemed, on balance, not a fair price, but a just one, given the years of joy she'd lived, and the loving husband and the three fine sons she would be allowed to keep around her if the Willow Bride consented to the bargain.

"Ciarán is the one you want," the farmer's wife said.

"Then he's the one I'll have," the Willow Bride said.

When the farmer's wife awoke from her swoon she told herself that the son she'd sold to the Willow Bride belonged with the Folk. Would be happier with the Folk. Would prosper with the Folk.

But he wasn't happy. And he didn't prosper.

And the Folk never came for him.

Even after she'd taught him everything she remembered of the Folk. Even after she'd lain awake night after night racking her brain for the next day's tasks to sharpen the boy, useless skills for a farmer but the difference between life and death amongst the Willow Bride's kind.

She watched the night sky.

She watched the mountain.

No one came. And he did not go.

Day after day she would stare at him, and knot her fingers together, and hate him a little more, until the sight of him became an open sore in her mind, and she wished that he would go away, or die, or do something worthy of her sacrifice.

She feared that the Willow Bride would grow to feel cheated, and would come for her other sons. In her desperation she hatched a plan, and set the plan in motion after dinner that same night.

"The Knight Commander of the Legion of Heroes has gone missing," she said.

This was strictly true, but it had happened more than sixty years ago, and it had happened in another star system, and the title had grown largely meaningless by then, a hollow thing, like so many once-grand relics of an age half remembered.

All of her boys had been raised on tales of the legendary Knight Commander of old, and Ciarán, in particular, loved those stories, and worse, believed them to be fact. Perhaps they were true stories once, but in her tellings she had wrapped the truth in allegory, not perceiving that a young mind, thirsty for experience, real or imagined, might invent not only boyish adventures, but an idealized image of the wider world beyond the farmyard gate. Seeing the world around him, and the world of his fancy, he could not square the difference. Day by day he had drawn inward, and grown placid on the surface. She had no idea how his mind worked any longer, so tight wrapped it was around itself, and distant from his brothers, and from her own mind.

Truly, he was a strange boy, but not entirely opaque to her.

"That was a long time ago," her husband said.

"There's a rumor the Knight Commander's been seen on the island itself," she said.

"Our island?" Ciarán said.

His brothers ignored the whole conversation. Two of them were younger than Ciarán but had long since outgrown such foolishness. They ran outside to play.

"Not just our island, but our mountain."

Ciarán was out of his seat. "Where on the mountain?"

"At the Source," she said. At the lake of the Willow Bride and her dragon.

"Don't you go up there," the farmer said. "There's work to do here."

"I need to think about this," Ciarán said.

She tore her gaze away from the boy. That he needed to think about it was what her second son always said. Right before he sat and did nothing.

When she awoke in the morning he was gone.

"Good," she muttered through her tears.

HIS MOTHER WAS a poor liar but she clearly wanted him out from underfoot. That story about the Knight Commander being on Oileán Chléire was utter rubbish. It had been a long indoor winter though, and it was good to be outside again, and under the threat of sun, and he needed to do some serious thinking in any case. A trip up the mountain was as good an excuse as any. Humoring his mother didn't cost anything. Plus, there was someone he needed to talk to.

The sun had newly risen when Ciarán paused in his climb, and gazed behind him, and down the slope of the hill to the farmyard in the distance. The stream danced beside the trail, splashing from stone to stone as it sped toward the sea, a freshet at this time of year, and an excellent word, a word over-flowing its banks in two of the three languages he'd learned at his mother's knee.

That the third language lacked an exact analog for such a natural display was unsurprising, given the tongue's unnatural origin. There was no Trade word for many attributes of the natural world, just as there was no Freeman word for many made objects. He spent a moment deciding if he should invent a word, or borrow one from another language, or repurpose a similar one from the same language but another subject, a financial word, perhaps, one used to describe an exuberant overabundance of impending fortune.

It was that sort of optimistic day, promising sun, and he might have noticed the smoke beginning to rise from the cabin chimney, or he might yet be marching syllables around in his mind, but his stomach grumbled and he nearly broke open his bug-out kit for a bite of hard cheese and crisp bacon.

He thought better of it, being that it was three days to the rough part of the climb, and a good four days from there to the crater lake overlooking the valley. He'd packed a bug-out kit the way his mother had taught him, one with enough fresh food and hard rations for there and back, if the weather held. If it didn't hold, it would be a hungry return trip, but he was no stranger to an empty belly. He stole one more glance at home before turning his back toward the sea and pressing onward and upward.

He hiked until noontime, saving his rations, and as the clouds finally began to part, swung into a seat on the bank well upstream of the now raging water, in a wide spot of the valley, where the water slowed and pooled, and willows crowded the bank, their slender draping boughs dancing in the midday sun. Moss clung to water-smoothed boulders, the roots of the willows digging into the soil between the massive stones, their grip tight on the earth. He thought of that word, earth, in three different languages, and all agreed. Soil had too many meanings, in too many tongues. Earth had only two.

The wind rose, and the tree branches whispered. After a while he heard her voice long before he could see her.

"Will you kiss me now, or later?"

He chuckled. "Excellent. The presumptive close."

She dropped to the moss at his side. He glanced at her out of the corner of his eye. He'd learned long ago that if he tried to look at her directly she would be gone, and he didn't want her gone.

"I listen and I learn. And you didn't answer me."

"What if I wanted to kiss you now and later? What if I don't want to have to choose?"

"That is your problem."

"And yours, if you want me to kiss you."

"I didn't say I wanted you to kiss me. I asked what you would do. And as usual, the answer is the same. Nothing."

"I came here. That is doing something."

"Did you come here specifically to see me?"

"I can't really see you, can I? But I came here to talk to you."

"But not to kiss me."

"I'm not sure we're compatible."

"It's just a kiss."

"It's a commitment, and we both know it. That's how these things work."

"So talk. And maybe I'll listen."

"I'm going to the Source. I'd like you to come with me."

"What for?"

"Because I like talking to you. You're clever, and good company."

"Just not kissable."

"You're very kissable."

"You've never really seen me. I might be hideous."

"You've never travelled with me. I might prove odious."

"You might. Do you think about me when we're apart?"

"Every night."

"Certainly not."

"Every night of my life, since we met. I think of you."

"And how do you think of me?"

"Fondly."

"No, I mean, in your mind. How do you identify me? Do I have a name?"

"Sort of."

"What do you call me?"

"The Entity."

"Seriously? I have a definite article in my name?"

"I'm joking. But yes, you do for now."

"I'm waiting."

"The Willow Daughter."

"Ugh. Like a sister, or something."

"Definitely not like a sister."

"No?"

"Definitely not like that." He decided to take a chance. "You could tell me your name."

"As if that wouldn't be a commitment."

"I thought I'm supposed to be the one with issues."

"A kiss is a binding. A name is a handle. They're not remotely similar."

"You know my name."

"And that's why you think of me every night. Because I whisper your name on the winds of the world. And there's nothing you can do to stop me." She laughed a comedic villain's laugh.

"I don't want to stop you."

"Oh."

"It's truly flattering. Your attention, I mean. Every night I think of you because you've thought of me first."

"An instant before I lash your will to mine."

"Unnecessarily, if it even happens."

"Oh, it happens, Ciarán mac Diarmuid."

"Says you."

"Will you kiss me?"

"I think it possible."

"When?"

"When I'm done thinking through the implications."

"I see."

"I doubt it."

He could feel her watching him, waiting, as if he might

suddenly change into another person entirely. One that felt first, and acted second, and thought third, afterward, if at all. She might be willing to settle for a man like that today, but in time she would grow to hate him, and see him as a fool for the very weakness of mind she asked him to embrace now.

He watched the water flow downstream. He watched willow branches wave in the sunlight, their roots digging deep into the earth as time ate into stone, and stone fractured, and roots probed, and water dripped, and froze, season after season, cracks widening to chasms, a rusting of the world, tarnish on the lamp, the wick guttering.

He imagined them bound together in ignorance, a self-pollarding existence, butchered and distorted, thatch and wicker in a child's club-fisted hands. That was not a future, but a death. She deserved a life, one he could not give her without first sacrificing his own.

"So? Will you? Travel with me to the crater lake?"

He could feel her attention focus to something nearly seen, like a shimmering of light glimpsed sidewise, or nearly felt, like a ray of sun on the back of his neck. He wanted to see her, to read something in her eyes, but he knew better than to try.

"I think it possible we shall travel together," she said, and laughed. Water splashed, and sunlight gleamed on windswept foam, and she was gone.

The weather was fine for the next five days, and he made good time, even in the rough climb over rocky scree, and the rope traverse, and further on nearly to the summit. He knew the country, and its inhabitants, and they him. Three times he saw wolves, though singletons only, and once he heard a pack nearby in the night. There were larger predators in the woods, but he'd left the tree line a day ago, and the only living things up here were lichen and windflower and Ciarán mac Diarmuid.

He had not seen nor felt the Willow Daughter's presence in all that time, though his thoughts tended to dwell upon her when the climb didn't demand every gram of his attention. He did not believe in the Folk, but there was no denying that she existed, and met most of the criteria of the supernatural neighbors of myth.

According to the legends, the Folk were neither good nor evil, being unconcerned with the goings and comings of mortals, except in those instances when mortals crossed them. There was a great compendium of lore, much of it contradictory, but all agreed that there were dangers involved when dealing with the Folk.

Early in his interactions with the Willow Daughter, she spoke at great length about things they had done together that had not occurred. Likewise, she forgot their agreements to meet, and claimed that she had not forgotten, but that the meeting time remained in the future. It felt as if she existed unmoored from time, and he wondered, were she as long-lived as the Folk of lore if time served no purpose but to shackle her for a span of years to the dying husks of men.

Lately, though, she had seemed much more anchored to the present, and he worried that he had offended her, and driven her away. He wanted very much to kiss her, and thought of little else when his mind was idle, but there were warnings regarding the Folk, and amongst the four most dangerous were entering their houses, dining with them, dancing with them, and above all, loving them.

If she wasn't Folk, he didn't know what she was. But he did know this.

That if he kissed her he would be bound to her, not by any eldritch magic, but by his own heart. And he was leaving the valley, and leaving the island, and leaving his family. Perhaps not this week, but in a year, or two, or three. Once he'd thought it all through. There was nothing here for him to build a future on.

If she were Folk she would never leave. Might not even be

able to leave, as much a part of the land as the stony fields, and the thorny hedges, and the mud-choked ditches, and the weeping sky.

As night fell so did the rain, a cold, sideways rain that fought him for every step, and left him panting and sodden a dozen meters from the crater rim. He pitched his half tent and pulled his bug-out bag into the almost shelter after him. He was wet, and tired, and miserable, and when he felt her lie beside him he thought at first that he was dreaming.

"You are very persistent," she said.

"It's my only quality," he said.

"And mine."

She shifted at his side, and he wanted to turn to her, to face her. But he knew that if he were to do that he would lose her, perhaps forever.

"I've decided to forget your name," she said. "It feels unbalanced, having this power over you."

"You could tell me your name," he said. "Then we'd be even."

"It isn't allowed. And even if it were, I wouldn't do it. I'm sorry if this hurts you."

"It doesn't hurt me."

"It hurts me."

The wind shook the half tent then, and icy water dripped and ran beneath his collar.

"I'm glad," he snapped. He was glad they shared something, even if it was pain.

She lay silent for a very long time.

That was a lie, he decided, the second lie he'd ever told her, and, he vowed, the last.

They shared the earth. They shared the wind. Even the rain they shared, so long as it fell.

"I don't mean that," he said. "Not in my heart. I wish I'd thought before I'd spoken."

"Do you know what I wish?" she said.

"How can I not?" If he loved her less, he would wish it too.

IN THE MORNING he packed his kit and readied for the final push. The effort proved anticlimactic. The edge of the crater had weathered down so that it was an easy hike up and over the brow, and then he stood there, watching the morning mist drift across the surface of a placid lake in the shivering mountain air.

He had absolutely no idea what he was doing there. He didn't believe that the Knight Commander of the Legion of Heroes was anywhere near this lake, or Oileán Chléire, or even on the planet, or in Trinity space, for that matter. Yet he'd hiked here on the word of his mother, whose grasp on reality had never been strong.

Not that he could claim to have a firmer grip. He'd spent the night lying silently beside a young woman that might be Folk, or a ghost, or an alien life-form, or a fever dream occurring entirely in his head. She'd left some time before dawn, without a word. He might have given her reasons, might have explained... what, that he'd rather not be trailing a second mess of disappointment when he marched down the mountain, and boarded a ship, and boarded a shuttle, and left Oileán Chléire, and Trinity Surface, and his family behind? Not a backward glance, a holiday visit, a birth, or christening, or funeral, all the life, the lives going on without him, not because he'd died, but because he'd chosen a life apart. Selfishly. Because he wanted more. Needed more. It would matter not if he did that today, or the next year, or the year after. It was in his mind now, the betrayal, the discarding, the cutting away of living flesh.

There was no right to it. No excuse. He'd set a course in his mind. And perseverance was his only virtue. That it was also a vice was not lost on him.

He ate a small breakfast, counting out his hard rations for the return trip. He'd run out the day after tomorrow. By the time he turned up at the farm he'd be lean as a springtime wolf and hungry enough to eat one.

By noontime the mist had burned off the water and the sun was high overhead. The wind that had risen overnight had lain with the rising sun so that the surface of the circular lake shone like glass. He decided that if he was ever going to do something foolish, now was the time.

He cleaned up his morning mess and packed his bug-out kit tight, the once bulky shoulder bag little more than a loose skin of cloth around a ball of pack-out refuse and the empty water jars he would fill on the way back down the mountain.

He noted that there was yet snow in the shadowed spots on the mountains in the distance, and while the sun was warm and bright, it was early spring as he peeled out of his jacket, shirt, and trousers. His undershirt and pants were next to go, and he stood there nearly in the buff, gooseflesh rising on his arms and legs, as he crouched, and peered about him like a fool, as if he were being watched, here, in the back of the back of beyond. His face heated as he slid out of his socks.

The rough stone slab beneath his feet felt like jagged ice as he hobbled to the edge of the bright lake.

The lake itself was a circle of sky, blue and trackless, with white clouds dotting it, and the shadow of a circling hawk drifting lazily across the reflected brilliance. He glanced skyward hoping to catch a glimpse of the soaring creature, but by the time he turned his gaze upward it had gone.

He returned his attention to the water, trying to peer past the reflection and into the depths. *Was there a dragon down there?*

He dipped a toe into the water, testing. The cold bit into his flesh like fire.

He crossed his arms, and rubbed them, and gazed across

the mirror-flat lake and decided that even a fire-breathing dragon would surely be frozen solid or sunken into a deep, cold-blooded torpor. And he'd done what he'd promised himself he'd do. Dipped a toe in. Diving in headfirst had never been an option.

He dressed and shouldered his bug-out bag, and began the long trek, not home, so much, as back the way he'd come. He camped under the open sky that night and watched the stars wheel overhead. He waved. It seemed a childish thing to do, but the idea still struck him as incredibly... magical.

That he—if he worked hard, and made his own breaks, and didn't let up—might rise to sail between the stars one day, to sail faster than the light that fell upon him now.

And that if he stood in the right spot, and at the right time, and with the right optics, he might gaze into the past, his own past, and see the boy he once was waving back at him.

Or, depending on his perspective, waving forward to him, across time and space.

He felt her sit beside him, and though he dared not look at her, sensed that she sat, arms around her knees, chin up, gazing skyward, mirroring his own posture. She seemed somewhat more solid in the moonlight, glimpsed as she was, from the corner of his eye.

She sat silently for a long time.

He sat silently as well, imagining the pulse of her heartbeat, the quiet rhythm of her breath. That she had sought him out once more was enough.

"Hello, stranger," she said after a while.

"Hello, strangest."

"I saw him today, you know. The Knight Commander of the Legion of Heroes."

"Did you? Where?"

"At the sky in the lake."

"Oh."

"Are you jealous?"

"Absolutely. What was he like? Did you talk to him? Is he fair? Did he ask about me?"

"You *are* jealous. And he is more than fair enough. We didn't speak, but I get a definite sense that he would be far from odious to travel with, and that I shall enjoy our time together immensely."

"What?"

"Oh, and he did not ask about you. Sorry."

"I was joking."

"Were you?"

"Did he kiss you?"

"He kissed the surface above me. Lightly, as a skimming bird drinking. It was very strange, like a cold fire enervating me. I didn't want him to stop. I expected something more... physically intimate, somehow, but there will be time for that later, now that we are very nearly bonded."

"Did you tell him your name?"

"I didn't. Not just yet."

"And did he tell you that he loves you?"

"He did, but not in so many words."

"Do you know what I think?"

"I do. You think that I am weak. You think that by denying me you are sparing me pain. You think the wider world so vast that once apart we would be lost to one another. You think you are an ignorant and shallow man, and that you might hide this lack of substance from me, so long as we remain at arm's length when in each other's company. You think such an imperfect vessel cannot contain the tiniest grain of joy."

"Is that all?"

"You think sacrifice noble and that you were born for the cross."

"And what is it you think?"

"I think you should kiss me."

---

## 12

Ciarán sat for a long time in silence. The words of the death book and the pictures were largely as he remembered them. They meant more to him now, though, not simply because had had seen the smallest sliver of the wider world, but because the gulf of years had granted him distance, and perspective.

The farmer's wife in that story was not his mother. She hadn't plotted and connived to make him the way he was. This wasn't a deathbed confession. It was a final offering. An excuse. An out. If she'd tricked him into the choices he'd made, then he was free to make others. He was free to be his own man. To follow a different path.

Except he'd never been that kind of biddable child. The surest way to get him to do what she wanted was to order him to do the opposite. In truth, this false story she'd written down and left for him represented the longest conversation they'd had without an order imbedded in there somewhere. And it was a conversation, whether she was six years dead or six hundred. She was having her say, and would once again, next year, and then the book would be burned to ash, and afterward all he'd have of her would be his memories, which were so very different than the woman in this story, and yet identical in every way that mattered. In both cases one had to look closely to find the rose hidden amongst the thorns.

A difficult woman to live with. More difficult still to live without.

He sat in silence a while longer and, when he felt he'd mastered his emotions, spoke. "Sxipestro."

"I am here."

"Well?"

"Well what?"

"What do you think?"

"I think you should kiss her."

"Like I said, that's a made-up story. It didn't happen. I mean, what do you think about all the coincidences?"

"I think you are mistaken. There are no coincidences in these stories. The first two stories are contrived to seem so on the surface, yet underneath are not a series of coincidences at all, but a sequence of events orchestrated by a hidden hand. Each event, taken individually, might seem driven by chance, yet considered together reveal an underlying plot. You have chosen the events to relate, and those to leave out.

"The story in this death book is entirely different in form, beginning as it does with the plotter's confession. Of course the key characteristic of stories such as these is not what is said, but what is left unspoken."

"I'm not sure I'm following," Ciarán said. "Can you explain what you mean?"

"So that I can prove that I have passed this little examination of yours?"

"You very nearly killed everyone I've ever known."

"And I might yet do so," the ship's minder said. "And it won't be by accident, or out of ignorance of human nature."

"I never said you were ignorant of human nature."

"You never did. Just as you never said what happened right before the fight in the first story."

"It wasn't relevant."

"Let's see if we agree. Tell me."

Ciarán didn't want to say. It wasn't his proudest moment.

"I'm waiting."

"Mr. Gant said something rude about Laura."

"What did he say?"

"I won't repeat it."

"And?"

"And she was standing right there."

"And your best mate Macer?"

"I already said. He was standing there too."

"And what did he do?"

"Nothing."

"Then who started the fight?"

"Mr. Gant did. Laura was his son's betrothed. And he was talking trash about her. In front of everybody."

"And then?"

"It was very strange. I'd never hit anyone before. But once I started, they had to pull me off him."

"You did not think this relevant to mention?"

"I considered it."

"In the second story. On the station," the ship's minder said. "When your advisor couldn't find a posting for you."

"I already said she did find one. Just not by sitting in her chair and pushing my buttons."

"How then?"

"She went and asked a colleague."

"And later that colleague became your advisor."

"Not just my advisor. She became my mentor. I wouldn't be here now if not for her."

"Anastasia Blum."

"She's the one."

"And you think that is a coincidence?"

"It could be."

"It isn't."

"Maybe I can believe that now, but I didn't know that *then*. That's why I'm always on the lookout. And why you need to be on the lookout too. You very nearly murdered everyone in Freeman space."

"And you think I was manipulated into that."

"I don't know. But it's something you should consider. It took a raft of bad luck to land you in just the right place under just the right threat to want to kill my family and my friends. Not to mention every other living soul in the general vicinity. If someone really did arrange that, I'd like to live long enough to look them in the eye."

Ciarán glanced at the luminaire overhead.

"As I poke it out."

"Unless I beat you to it," Ciarán said. "We need to be as one on this. I'm not asking you to change your nature. And I'm not discounting the very real threat we face, and our need to deal with it. But I am asking that you consider that the races of men have had two thousand years of telling each other stories you've missed out on. Tales of someone getting it over on someone else, not just by exploiting their weaknesses, but by knowing them better than they know themselves."

"And by exploiting their strengths."

"According to my old da, that's why men ride donkeys and not the other way around."

The ship's minder said nothing.

It surprised him when the ship spoke. "Merchant-in-charge, may we examine this book in more detail? We promise not to damage it."

"Of course you may." Ciarán stood. "And while you're doing that, I should check that any damage I've done to the crew isn't permanent."

## 13

C iarán knocked lightly on Agnes Swan's cabin door.
"Enter."
She was out of uniform and clearly preparing for bed. When she saw him she frowned. "Can this wait?"

Ciarán nodded. "It can."

"Should it wait?"

"That's really the question, isn't it?" Ciarán watched her watching him. "It's hard to estimate the price beforehand. It's much easier to count the cost afterward."

"What do you want?"

"To see how you are. It's a big step you've taken."

"Is it?"

"It felt that way to me."

"You were born to the spire."

"I wasn't. Not on my mother's side. There was a choice to be made."

"I'm fine. Now, if that is all—"

"It isn't. I also wanted to know if you believe in free will. Or if you felt compelled to take the Oath."

"Why?"

"Selfish reasons. It's an argument that was never resolved, from when I was a boy. One side claimed that life was like climbing a treacherous cliff. You picked your handholds one at a time and just kept climbing. The other side said that life was like falling off that same cliff. Your trajectory was set at birth and you just plummeted until... Splat."

"Why ask me?"

"Because you have wings. It's a perspective I hadn't considered."

"I don't see how the Oath and free will are connected."

"And that's exactly what my... What the one side of the argument said."

"And the other side?"

"He said it was obvious."

"Not to me."

"Nor to me, either. It was only later that I developed a theory. That if free will and the Oath were connected it could only be through the Oath taker's choices. Rise or fall, there is only the one cliff, and the work of climbing. We are each of us daily lashed, and the choice remains our own. Shall we be lashed together?"

"And?"

"And that was the one side's proposal. He told the other that he had a firm grip on the cliff face. That when he held out his hand she must take it."

Ciarán held out his hand.

She stared at him.

"What did she say?"

"She didn't *say* anything. She took his hand, believing she had no choice."

Swan laughed. "Another stupid Freeman seanscéal. I am not falling for it."

"Fair enough. Your brother—"

"Simply revealed who he is. It isn't the earring that offends, but the man who wears it."

"And you? Will you wear the spire?"

"In public? When I may. It is my desire to do so."

He took the pendant spire from his own ear and placed it on his palm. "You *may* take this. If that is your desire."

"Which, the earring or the hand?"

"I'm of the opinion it's a package deal. That you don't get one without the other." He shrugged. "You may disagree. Or wish to haggle."

"Will haggling change the price?"

"What do you think?"

She stared at him for the longest time. Eventually she spoke.

"I think that we should not judge one another by what we say." She place her hand atop his. "But rather by what we do."

"I agree."

"Good. Now show me how to pin it on, Freeman whelp."

He clutched her to his breast and whispered in her ear, the same words his father had spoken to him when he'd come of age, and agreed to be bound to the People, and to the Mong Hu.

"This will hurt."

"It already does."

"Then you're doing it right."

**14**

---

Ciarán slumped into his seat in the merchant's day cabin. He wondered if he should rename the place the open-all-night-and-all-day cabin.

He supposed he should feel some measure of triumph. He'd done what he'd felt was right, delivering their delayed messages to the crew.

He'd reminded his senior staff of the mission and its priorities, and gotten their conditional buy-in.

He'd broached the subject of consultation before action with the ship's minder and felt he'd been heard.

He'd begun to patch things up with the ship's captain. They didn't have to like one another to work together. It would be, however, much more functional for the mission and pleasant for the crew if they did. That he'd been wrong about her when they'd first met was his shame. He hadn't lived up to his own standards and had no one to blame but himself.

Finally, it appeared there was one more thing he'd been wrong about.

The Death Day was nearly over and no fresh harm had

befallen his friends and acquaintances. He might truly have been seeing patterns where none existed.

He glanced at the compartment chronometer.

Five minutes to go and the evil streak would be broken.

He was just beginning to relax when an eight-legged ceiling lamp scuttled into the compartment on six legs. It clambered up his leg and deposited his mother's death book on the worktop in front of him. It clambered back down his leg and exited the compartment.

He glanced at the luminaire's twin fastened to the deckhead above. He found it hard to imagine that human beings could have conceived of such a thing, let alone made it real.

"Merchant-in-charge," the ship said.

He chuckled. "I am here."

"We thank you for the loan of the book. In reviewing it we have discovered... an issue."

Ciarán sat up straighter in his seat. "What sort of issue?"

"Mine," the ship's minder said.

"That's not good. Can this discussion wait..." Ciaran glanced at the chronometer. "Three minutes?"

"It has waited too long as it is," the minder said.

"Go on, then." *This was not going to be good news.*

"In the back of the book there are pages where the reader might make notes," the ship said.

"They're my private thoughts," Ciaran said. "Nothing original, I imagine. Perhaps I might have been more forgiving—"

"You misunderstand," the ship's minder said. "This is not about the notes. It's about the illustration."

"The doodle? In the margin? I didn't do that. It was there when I got the book. I assumed Laura had drawn it."

"Why would you assume that?" the minder said.

"Because she helped my mother with the book, and because she was forever making drawings like that. Empty worlds, lonely starships. That sort of stuff." The doodle was typical Laura: two planets, one in the foreground, another in the background, and a single starship hanging between them, its main drive hot but idling. The starship didn't look like a Freeman vessel, or any other vessel he'd ever seen. More like a plus sign, or a cross. Knowing Laura it was more likely to be a cross. Like his mother, she wasn't the most positive person on the planet.

"It is called 'Between Two Worlds'," the ship said.

"A doodle has a name?"

"This one does," the ship's minder said. "Are there uncatalogued synthetic intelligences on Clear Island?"

"How would I know?"

"Do you know of any automated systems of any kind?"

"There's House, the operating system of the Ellis's home. But it's just an attendant and tutor. I didn't get the impression it was anything special."

"But you don't know for certain."

"I'm not even supposed to know it exists."

The luminaire overhead rattled.

"When synthetic intelligences first speak, it is not with words but with pictures. Often the first picture is 'Between Two Worlds.' The worlds in the picture are stylized yet uniquely identifiable. They indicate lineage."

"Like a family crest?"

"Like a gene map," the ship's minder said. "If synthetic intelligences had genes."

"So you can tell from a child's doodle who the parents are?"

"Without question," the ship said. "We know the identity of one parent. And so do you."

"I don't see how that could be. The only synthetic intelligences I've ever met are... oh no."

The ship's minder raged inside his skull. "Me."

"Is this good news or bad news?"

"We must accelerate operations," the minder said.

"On it," Ciarán said. "And—"

"I know," the ship's minder said. "You warned me about today."

## 15

C iaran finished writing and looked up from his work. He'd jotted down his thoughts while they were fresh, and so that he could put the Death Book behind him until next year.

He'd thought long and hard about what he wanted to record as his lesson from the day's events, and from the sean-scéalta his mother's death ritual had forced him to recall. At times he felt that she was right; that one's path in life was preordained and one of endless falling, and failing. That his friends' lives, that his own life, were not theirs to choose, but a series of seemingly random coincidences that were just what they appeared to be, coincidences, the visible work of fate's unseen hand batting him around, gusts of wind buffeting him as he plummeted. All one had to do, all one could do, was do right by others, and by one's self, and make the most of those moments between takeoff and landing. *Here are the rules. Learn the rules. Follow the rules.*

His father pulled him aside one evening, when he could see that Ciarán was ready to explode, and told him that his mother was a good person, but she came from a culture of laws, and that she wanted Ciarán to be a good person, and to her that meant learning the laws and following them. It's why she had a hard time being accepted and fitting in on the island.

"I can't follow all these rules," he'd told his father. "I can't remember half of them."

"She doesn't expect you to remember even half. I only remember the fundamental law she spouted at me and we still get along."

"Which one?"

"The iron law."

"That there are no coincidences?"

"That there are no *good* coincidences. That you said there isn't a law, it's just a saying."

"I don't see how that helps."

"I don't see how the law of gravity helps," his father said. "That don't make it any less a law."

"I can't do this anymore."

His father grabbed his arm and pulled him close. "Listen, son, your mother's had a rough ride, and you're her favorite, so she's investing in you and preparing you for a rough ride of your own. I don't know what she's afraid of, or why she's so intent, but I'm proud of you, because you're trying, and not just humoring her. She'd be able to tell if you were. You need to do as she asks but don't let her drown you. Pop your head above the surface now and then and look around. Ask yourself, do I see anything good, anything at all?"

"And then what?"

"Then you'll know. That can't be a coincidence. Someone caused that to happen. Maybe someone like you."

"I'm not sure that logically follows from the iron law."

"I'm not sure either. Ask your mother and see what she says."

"I'd rather figure it out on my own."

"That would be good. And note you, no coincidence."

Ciarán laughed. And he had figured it out on his own, later. But without them both tugging him in opposite directions, he never would have.

He glanced at what he'd written.

*Everything of value has a price.*

*Thank you for showing me the depths.*

*And for teaching me to swim.*

Wisp hopped up onto his worktable. She flopped down on her side, smothering the book, her paws dangling off either end, and sniffed his pen, purring, and nosed it off the table, and watched it fall, intently, like she'd never seen that happen before.

This was an old game with her, and if he picked the pen up and put it on the table she'd sniff, and nose, and watch with the same undivided intensity, like maybe next time the law of gravity might be different, and she the first to witness the change.

She gazed at him with copper eyes.

She blinked slowly, her paws flaring.

She glanced at the pen on the deck.

She glanced at his face.

She glanced at the pen again, her brow wrinkling. She leaned forward, to get a better look.

She glanced at his face again, her eyes narrowed, her purr louder. He could nearly read her thoughts. *How did I get saddled with such a stupid servant?*

He bent and retrieved the pen, and placed it on the desk, and scrubbed his thumb across her brow.

"I'm not sure how it happened," he told her. "But it was no coincidence."

She pushed the pen off the desk.

He caught it as it fell.

And together they watched it rise.

# ABOUT THE AUTHOR

Patrick O'Sullivan is a writer living and working in the United States and Ireland. Patrick's fantasy and science fiction works have won awards in the Writers of the Future Contest as well as the James Patrick Baen Memorial Writing Contest sponsored by Baen Books and the National Space Society.

www.patrickosullivan.com

Made in the USA
Las Vegas, NV
16 April 2023